OSAWATOMIE

OSAWATOMIE

A Novel

RANDY MICHAEL SIGNOR

Parts of *Osawatomie* first appeared in a shorter form in several different publications. The 1960 material largely appeared as "The Girl and the Fire and the Buick" (though under a slightly different title) in *Black Clock #3,* Spring 2005; portions of the mid-1950s material appeared as "Osawatomie" in *The Midwesterner,* February 1997; and a long story based upon the 1850s material, called "The Gypsies," first appeared in *The Long Story,* Spring 2007.

Cover designed by Kent Johnson/Massive Graphics

ISBN-13: 978-1-63505-567-2
LCCN: 2017900871

MCP Books
2301 Lucien Way #415
Maitland, FL 32751
407·339·4217
www.MCPBooks.com

Distributed by Itasca Books

Printed in the United States of America

First Edition

Publisher's Note

This is a work of fiction and while some historical events and figures are used, anyone reading this for history will go away confused and unhappy. I made this up. Residents of Osawatomie will recognize that several buildings have been moved to suit my purposes. Little of this happened and what did happened differently for sure. Think of this as a truthful alternative telling and you'll enjoy it more.

For my mother Joan Signor, who gave me the world; for Mrs. M—Geneva Mendenhall—who opened my eyes to it all; and for Jane Levine, who makes my world spin.

1960

John David

We started out with the girl in back, me up front, and Woody driving, but she wanted to talk so much we stopped and I got out and she tilted the seat forward, crawled around it and hopped over next to Woody, a nice wide smile and her already picking up where she left off before we stopped, some more jabber about her brother in jail for something he said, and her needing to collect on some money owed down where we lived. I climbed back in and slammed the door, and she gave me a quick look, and finished the story, her head bobbing side to side, punctuating the end with another big smile, showing very white teeth framed with bright red lips and dark negro skin.

We'd become friends you might say, standing on the sidewalk about four, five doors up from the burlesque, where you could see the great Muehlebach Hotel, where we knew Pendergast gangsters once lounged around in black pinstriped suits and big wide-brimmed hats. Story was some of Pendergast's gang secretly lived down in Osawatomie and commuted into the city, which seemed funny— did they kiss their wives on the forehead and then head off to KC, the *Times* tucked under their arms?

Woody and I'd cruised up to see the girly show and were standing there getting our story straight when this negro girl came out of nowhere and scared the bejesus out of me, honest, I jumped six inches and I know I made a noise of some kind.

Hi, she said. My name's Dorthea, what's yours? And the first of those great smiles shined on her face. It just seemed so infectious, you'd catch it from her even on a poor day.

I told her mine and Woody said his, though I could tell he thought about it for about the time it'd take to run through a couple made-up names he must have rejected. We all beamed at each other for a few seconds, though what was on Woody's face could not accurately be called beaming and then Dorthea wondered if we might buy her a drink, she was kind of low on funds and extra thirsty on this hot night.

We could toast Senator Kennedy, going to be the president, she said, be lots of changes then.

I couldn't argue about Kennedy or the heat. The young senator's promise had an elevated ideal that seemed airy and like something that couldn't be broken; and it was one of those summer nights when the night temperature was higher than most place's regular days. You just sweated through your clothes as soon as you moved a muscle, did anything at all, even driving a car with the windows wide open. Concentrating on something as simple as making a plan made me sweat, I felt a little self-conscious, my sweating and talking to this pretty negro girl.

Which I had no problem with, since, like Woody, I'd grown up in Osawatomie, where John Brown was from, the famous abolitionist and martyr for the negro slaves, that John Brown, captured at Harper's Ferry. We lived on Brown Street for a while and then, later, another house that was backed up against John Brown Memorial Park where we played baseball and tag and hide-and-seek.

Talk in our family was we had Brown blood. My mama showed me something that proved we were Browns. It made me proud when I considered it, and gave me something to live up to, a way of behaving that seemed modeled on something bigger than myself. It also was about all the fame we could claim.

We went to school with negroes our whole lives, and we didn't mind them none, being just another part of the bigger picture of our youth. It wasn't something we really talked about, though I had my

own feelings about it, from having negro friends in school. Sharon
Marie's face filled my mind.

So, you boys gonna buy me a drink, she asked.

Sure, I said, Woody mumbling, yeah, that'd be okay. His voice
lacked the kind of enthusiasm you'd want on such an enterprise but
he didn't squawk any more than that.

Well, she said, let's pop in here, her eyes cutting to a place right
behind us I hadn't noticed before, concentrating as we were on our
burlesque plans. I seen you out here, trying to figure out what to do,
I could tell, she said.

What was you talking about, she continued.

Nothing, just what we were gonna do, I said. Woody was inven-
torying the posters that covered the bar's front window. Fight posters,
a couple roller derby, quarter midgets on oval dirt tracks.

Thinking of taking in the burly-cue? she said.

Well, yeah, I guess, sure.

Well, I don't see you looking like the Jewel Box type, she said,
what looked like a wink joining the smile. The Jewel Box was a place
a few blocks further on where men dressed like women danced and
waited on tables and it was the fallback choice for guys who'd said it
was funny and no one got queer with them. I was pretty sure Woody's
list of fallback plans didn't include the Jewel Box, no matter how
funny guys'd said it was; that's why we had to get our stories straight.

Let's have that drink, whatcha say, she said, stepping on my
answer, which was okeydokey with me, not knowing what to say to
her, just meeting and all, and only about a half-stammer away from
talking directly about naked girls dancing on stage. I barely talked
about sex with Woody and we talked about almost everything, but
mostly I guess that would fall into the category of wishful thinking
or even trying to pass off completely made-up stuff as things we
actually did.

I was a virgin, I guess you'd say, but on the lookout to change
that my first opportunity.

I did not say that aloud. I don't know if I even thought it then, I'm just letting you know now, so you follow why I was so shy with this girl.

I had no idea what I was doing and I was pretty certain Woody was a few steps behind me, kind of gone dull of a sudden.

Well, we hadn't been, I said. To the burlesque, before tonight.

Said this real casual-like, see the burlesque, see the new horror movie, eeny-meeny, miney-mo, whichever.

You ain't never seen no women naked? Her eyes out big, like you look at the six-legged pig at the county fair, but that sweet smile cutting away any edge you might normally suspect.

I guess I haven't, I said, craning my neck around, finding Woody, bringing up the rear as we trailed into the bar, a long, narrow, dark room, booths on one side, stools down a dark wood bar on the other, aisle between. We walked by about a dozen men lined up on the stools, a couple men and women in booths, maybe two negroes for every white, took a booth about two thirds back.

I sat next to Dorthea. Woody was across, but down at the same end as Dorthea, kind of scrunched down, maybe so's he could play footsie with her, from how they each were sitting.

The air was thick with blue smoke and smelled fruity, like someone had spilled a bottle of perfume except under the sweetness was some sharp things, piss or vomit or sweat. I decided the perfumy smell was no accident and it was doing us all a favor.

We all sort of wiggled a little, getting adjusted, passing looks back and forth, no one saying anything. She wore a sleeveless dress, with flocks of bright red cardinals on a cream background, and I remembered her heels were red as well. Her bare arms looked as smooth as polished wood. Woody had on some clean Levi's with two-inch rolled cuffs and a white T-shirt his mom must have bothered to iron. I had on my new khakis and a white short sleeve shirt. We all should've been as crisp as new money, except for the heat so I guess it was like money that had been left in your pants and gone through the laundry.

After we settled in, she lurched up, leaned way over me, toward the bar, her heat rising into my face, called out loud, Archie, three here.

You got money? Archie yelled back.

She drew back a little, rolled some toward me, our faces real close together. I could smell her breath. Sweet but mediciney. Her eyes were almost closed. Her lips parted, her tongue peeked out. She whispered, you got this covered, lover?

I nodded, afraid to say anything with her leaning into me.

She twisted back, away, yelled at Archie over the top of the booth, bring fucking drinks, Archie. You know what I like.

That was not talk I heard every day, especially not in Osawatomie, from a girl. My face must have registered several degrees of disbelief. Woody's eyes bounced from her to me, just as surprised, doing something to his frown, sent some of it off somewhere, but only for a minute.

I saw Archie looking through the haze, sorting out the bodies. He was a big man, tall and heavy, hanging out over a folded bruised apron around his waist, his shirt dark from sweat. He dried off his hands on the apron and something flickered over his face, there and gone in a blink.

He brought drinks, three tall glasses half filled with something dark, with some ice cubes and a lemon slice hanging on the rim.

Archie said a sum. I pulled out my billfold, gave him a bill.

There'll be more, Dorthea said. Run a tab. You can see he's got it to pay.

Archie took his time running this through his head, looking at Dorthea, at me.

He shrugged and left, my bill back on the tabletop. Dorthea smiled like she'd just won her favorite Cracker Jack prize.

See, she said, we gonna have ourselves a time.

What is this stuff, asked Woody, dipping his head close to his drink, taking a sniff.

Rum and Coke, she said. A genuine tropical drink, cool you right off, hot shot.

1954

Mama talked about when she was young, finishing up high school down in Sedan and Mother Dawson, her great-great grandmama, just shy of one-hundred, took her aside and told her how she, my Mama, was her favorite, how she loved her even better than her own daughter, Mother Oldfather, and how she wanted Mama to do something special for her.

Mama asked what, and Mother Dawson said she wanted to dictate her memories. She had some things to say and she wanted Mama to write it down exactly the way she told it—that part was important—and Mama was the only one of her kin she could trust to do it right.

Of course, Mama said. She'd be delighted. About everything delighted Mama, at least until she got older and saw things weren't going to turn out the way she'd dreamed.

So they started getting together every morning that spring before Mama went off to school and before much else was going on. They'd meet in Mother Dawson's room which had been added on some years earlier when she'd moved in with my mama's family. The room was barely bigger than her bed, an old wooden and cane rocker, and a chest of drawers she said had been in the family since before they'd moved to Kansas, since before she could remember. The room was attached to the back of the house right up against the kitchen, so she'd open her door and be right there in the middle of the house and all its morning noise.

Mother Dawson talked and my mama wrote exactly what she heard. She even underlined certain things when Mother Dawson's voice seemed to add emphasis so that everything would be just right. Mother Dawson checked what Mama wrote the first few days but when she saw that what was written was what she'd said she more or less stopped peeking over her shoulder except occasionally, just to keep Mama on her toes, she said. She liked doing that, keeping people on their toes. Been doing it all her life, she said. It was her job and her duty and her mission, was what she said.

I heard about all this much later, of course. Mama talked about Mother Dawson as if she'd been some kind of prairie saint, or at least someone who'd done some special things in her life and deserved for that reason if nothing else to be revered and honored and her memory kept alive, which was why Mama would drag out those handwritten notebooks and read from them to us from time to time. The notebooks were old and brittle and the pages yellow or even brown and the ink sometimes faded to the point were you just had to guess what had been written there, her school-girl penmanship its only saving grace, those curlicues as graceful and round as stones worn perfectly smooth by some spring creek.

The one thing I learned for sure, though, was that Mother Dawson knew a hundred-plus years ago more than anyone ever thought, and she knew more than anyone I've met or known in my life. Her story is like a big, complicated painting that you can study on for years and years and see new things as the light hits the paint from different angles.

She kept her words in her head for all those years until she made my Mama write them down, just the way she wanted them. That's the way I'll remember them, words layered over other words on more words until she used them all up and her story was whole.

Mother Dawson died almost eight months to the day after she finished her dictation; she'd initialed the last page and had said to Mama it was a faithful transcription, and how pleased Mama had been to draw that praise.

Mama's stories always started with a reminder about how our family had been there at the beginning, from those first days when no more than a half-dozen families had staked out land in the broad river plain where Pottawatomie Creek and the Osage River joined, and called it Osawatomie, though we were in truth staked out along Mosquito Creek, one of many little creeks that fed into the larger rivers.

Then the story would commence, this evening's history lesson, the voice of my great-great-great grandmama. It became, over time, the same voice, Mama's and Mother Dawson's, whose I'd never in real life heard since she died some years before my birth.

SPRING-SUMMER/1854

From my earliest memories Simon held me captive. Part of it was that when I looked into his pale blue eyes I saw myself, even too much of myself. I always knew I knew him as well as I knew myself; perhaps, given everything, better than I knew myself.

If I had questions or doubts or uncertainties about myself or some part of the world, I only had to look into Simon's heart to know what I felt about it. Somehow the view into him was easier than the view into my own heart. He was from the beginning my touchstone, even my compass, as together we completed something whole, something halved and now, the two of us, rejoined.

It pleased me that as my brother he'd always be in my life. It was a simple fact I accepted as one of my base truths.

Everything after came from that.

Simon was my favorite, but my heart melted a dozen times a day for Jonah, though there's no denying his being the baby had something to do with it. He'd been bounced like a ripe melon all the way from Tennessee and I swear he cried hardly at all, even the time I dropped him in some river we forded when a wagon wheel hit a rock and it jarred me enough I bit my tongue and then our brother William yipped and threw himself into the brown water and came up thrashing and holding Jonah, water running off him and his soaked blanket still bundled around him like a shell. Jonah looked at me, wide wide eyes and his little mouth made a round cave and then he waved his arms and squinted and broke into baby giggles.

I made a fuss over switching out his wet wrapping for a dry one, rubbing him and tickling him and forcing myself to laugh with him.

I was extra careful after that, my eyes on the lookout for rocks and ruts and general trouble.

So Jonah was my weakness, I guess one of many, but if any one of us had something inside that could someday erupt and harm us all it was Simon and I kept one eye on him no matter what. Every day he was alive and we all lived together I could tell you where he was and usually what he was doing or certainly supposed to be doing. I'd find some way to check on him and I got so I could keep track of him without him much knowing it, I'm pretty sure of that. He sure never said anything to me about it, that's the truth, so he didn't know or he didn't care and the point is that I saw him at his natural best which was hardly good at all too much of the time.

Sometimes it seemed I couldn't get enough of that boy; even merely watching him from aways lifted my spirits.

William, the oldest, performed those duties as expected of oldest sons. They carried on best, my guess because as joined with Papa and Mama, the first, there is remembered strength from the solid tripartite base. The Holy Trinity on earth. Each child after is one step removed from their hearts, though the last is always as unique as the first, for reasons similar because the last completes the circle started by the first, and different because the last can never know what the first did and paid for and learned in a way the last didn't.

The best way to understand Drury would be to consider him a pretend version of William. He was caught twixt admiring and resenting, and when it wore him out I swear he'd start twitching, first around his mouth and then it'd spread like one of them poison ivies, little jerks and ticks here and there, plus sometimes you'd get a smell coming off him.

Middle boys—like Simon—well, they're a tossup, you just never know how they'll turn out, the full range, of course, between the bookend children, but more likely to be something all their own, less like the parents than either first or last. They are what truly makes a large family interesting.

Simon lived with a fever that made him restless but gave him a kind of flare, inflaming his organs so that he lived like a fancy St.

Louis gambler. I don't mean his clothes, although anyone would tell you that he dressed nice enough, given what we had to wear. He took care of his clothes and kept his Sunday Meeting suit wrapped in a piece of burlap he'd carefully cleaned before using it to protect his only suit, a suit I should add that had been worn by his two older brothers. Mama repaired it and re-sewed its seams and hems and darned its wear spots and Simon intended to pass it along as whole as he received it. And when he wore it he looked taller and more puffed up and he walked a little more certainly.

But we were all of us Papa's and Mama's children, as stubborn and tough as mule sinew but as tender in our hearts as a fat house cat. Papa's people had come over from England a generation before and he was born in eastern Tennessee, his daddy a poor scrubland farmer whose many failures shaded Papa's picture of the world. Papa was wiry from a lifetime of long days, joining his brothers and sister in his daddy's fields, each winter a miserable contest between what they grew over the summer and the thawing of the ground for the spring planting. Meals in late winter or early spring were often little more than small bits of chewy squirrel and some potatoes that had more eyes than a woods full of crows. Papa said they joked they were just a day or two away from stone soup.

Mama met Papa one morning when they were in town with their folks, she the shy one standing by the general store's open door, doing her best to stay out of the others' way, Papa almost as shy having shuffled himself into a corner near the door as well, the two of them stealing glances of each other, one set of eyes downcast, then up, meeting, the other's eyes then breaking, studying the nails in the floor planking.

If either one had been even a smidgeon more shy, I would not be here, but one—Papa says him, Mama says her—said something or coughed or muttered, and the other said, What? as though there had in fact been a word uttered under the din of townspeople bargaining with the shop owner.

Mama's family had just settled in the area and she knew no one and she had not yet started school. When she did there was Papa two rows away at his wooden desk, his hands clasped politely on top, his eyes focused on the brand-new blackboard and Mrs. Smithson dressed head to toe in black, only a white collar disturbing her bleak dignity.

Their eyes continued their dance and at recess Papa managed to greet Mama and offer her a smile. It was, she later said, the smile that won her over.

Over the next two years they became friends though lord knows it was a friendship rooted in country courtesy, each sentence escorted by a polite Miss or Sir, blushing cheeks and neck, and silences that seemed to trip together, bringing another smile or even an embarrassed giggle. Everyone else knew what was going on long before Mama and Papa admitted anything to themselves.

They were barely in their middle teens but when school let out at the end of the second year, they asked their parents for their blessings, which were granted, and they married.

They rented a parcel of land near Papa's family, a tiny log cabin set in its middle and a small, occasionally dry creek that ran diagonally through their land. They worked hard but the land was rugged and strewn with rocks of every size and three of the first four years the spring rains came too early, the summer heat too late, and storms rolled through like stampeding cattle.

William was born a year after the wedding, just in time to take Mama out of the summer fields. Drury showed up barely ten months later. Mama was sick much of Drury's first two years, the doctor could only shrug but he encouraged her to give her childbearing a break and so I wasn't born until almost three years later, followed by Simon, and then a much longer break before Baby Jonas appeared.

Mama said no more and took to consulting with some older women who lived outside of town and who gave her potions that did what they were supposed to do because Mama did not get pregnant again.

The thing going on that colored our daily lives was the constant news about Missouri raiders and the free-staters, riders ambushed from thorny ravines, settlers pulled from their homes and hung, horsemen galloping through town, tossing torches into stores, shooting up the newspaper offices, pistol shots exchanged from across ridges. On more than one trip into town I witnessed men shouting at other men, the women spinning on their heels, grabbing their children and heading back to the store or their wagons.

We had come from Tennessee, Papa said to find a new home, but truth be known, the move had been sponsored to aid the South's desire to win Kansas—the Kansas-Nebraska Act threw the territory up for grabs, free or slave, hold a vote on it. It was a big plus that Papa had two grown sons to bring along with him and another on his way, Simon aspiring to elbow into that group.

But we'd never owned slaves and Papa took the offer because it seemed the only chance to better our lives. We hadn't had much luck back home, our small farm there impossibly rocky and steep and it seemed like every year hard rainstorms washed away our crops. Combine that with general bad luck and a chance to go west and grab some free land in a territory that was flatter and the soil rich for growing corn and grains, room for some cows, couple horses, it was our dream revived.

Here cottonwoods marked the lazy creeks and rivers as they ran crookedly southeast. Persimmon and live oak and walnut trees grew in distended shapes like fat fingers following, generally, the wind's carrying of seeds; at times fanning out over a flat plain, at other times narrowing to a small stand of young saplings braving once barren ground.

Sunflower patches sprinkled the prairie and their raised faces followed the sun across its broad arc. The prairie here was less flat than rolling, like a quilt after a restless night's sleep.

There weren't any roads to speak of and everything then was a lot rougher and denser, more raw. We were the first in all history to live on that land in a regular way and make it support us season after season, so it looked the way it had looked since it was created, waving straw-colored grasses, trees that in spring windstorms loose clouds of ghost-white flowers, chicken hawks big as barn cats and as graceful in flight as martins.

When we first arrived, everything was new and unmarked and no mistakes had been made. All that we did was the first time, for us and the land, and it was our prayer we would not fail each other. We'd come out here because another season back there would have cost too much, so here we were, seemingly fresh and scrubbed free of our failures, new people joining with a new land.

We had high hopes.

And we weren't here for no slaves, neither. We were here for us. Our hearts belong to the land and not to anyone's ideas.

We did not preach on these things in our home but it so filled up people's lives around here it crept into things anyway. We talked about the weather and how the work was going, the crops, noting signs that Papa always read positively, more weather talk, made plans for the next day, if someone had gone somewhere or someone had stopped by. Supper was when we heard about neighbors or just tales about what was happening in Lawrence and Palmyra and Hickory Point and around. It seemed to me the free-staters were running things and it was the border ruffians who were stirring things up.

Papa did not encourage talk of beatings or killings or such. Nor did Mama, but all the boys bubbled with it and almost each night one or more of them said something.

It was so much around us I felt drenched with it. Every dirt devil or rider four ridges away sent my heart thumping in my chest. Simon told me it was all they talked about when Papa wasn't around.

1954

I was one of a dozen or so Cub Scouts playing through our regular Tuesday after-school meeting. Woody's mama was there with us in the snow-covered city park, herding us from one winter activity to another, the den mother with her charge of cubs. We'd started out observing nature in winter: icy limbs, snow crystals, frozen membranes like stiff handkerchiefs draped over brown or gray stubble; and then we'd made snowmen, snow angels, used twigs to write our names in the snow before we shuffled off toward the park exit in a winding line.

We were tired, trudging our way out of the park toward Woody's home across Main Street. We started to pass by the fountain, shut off since fall, the water in the large basin now frozen. Granite-lined, about forty feet in diameter, its glassy surface a shiny pinkish gray in the afternoon winter light, with flattened patches of snow scattered around like scraps of paper.

The twins, Brad and Lonnie, and I fell behind the others, behind Woody's mama breaking trail ahead. We darted over to the frozen fountain to skate on our shoes, three of us there at the edge, about to hop over, when Woody's mama called back, hey don't go out there. I don't know how strong's that, and the twins stopped but I vaulted over, my leap enough to send me gliding across the mottled gray surface, and then suddenly up to my waist in ice water. I remember the dreamy shock and gasping for air.

Woody's mama was there instantly and with the help of the twins hauled me out of the water, which was only a couple feet deep. I was hurried across the street and into Woody's house. My pants had turned slushy and then, while I walked, thickened into a layer of cakey, cracked ice. I was stripped and dried off, wrapped in thick white towels, and put into a chair in the kitchen to wait for Mama to come and get me, bring a change of dry clothes.

That was the first time I fell through ice. The second time wasn't for another year, the year everything happened. Eisenhower was deep into his first term. It was the year someone set fires. One of those fires killed a baby, the cousin of a classmate.

No one knew who did it.

It was also the year Mama thought that a pair of skates she'd had since high school might fit me. They did. Ice skating was to be Mama's latest device to get me out of the house after school.

Meek Grade School held down one entire end of the block between Brown and Pacific avenues, on the opposite end of the block as the high school with the city library in between, and was one of those old dark-brick schools, two floors, four rooms to a floor, one to a corner, doorways opening onto a large central hall that held the water fountains. Long narrow coat closets separated the rooms and opened onto the hall at one end and into the classroom at the other end.

Each classroom had a set of tall, wide sash windows along one wall, and the windows rattled furiously in rainstorms on spring afternoons, lights flickering, failing, Mrs. Friedman calming us with jokes or perhaps by reading, our heads rested on our folded arms on dark wood desks permanently bolted to the floor, the kind of desks that had benches that folded up, built-in pencil trays centered at the top, holes for bottles of ink, and fancy grillwork along the sides. The blackboard was black, the chalk tray was wide and deep and had a permanent film of white dust and I loved the smell of the chalk dust when I erased words or a division problem.

Meek was where I met Jaimie.

From kindergarten through sixth grade, Jaimie and I were the two fastest kids in school. One day he was fastest, one day I was. The colored kid and the white kid, out there on the big side playground—more rock and bare dirt and black cinders than grass—running after kids or from kids, every day a game of tag, we either the last to get caught or the ones doing some easy trolling, reeling in all the slower kids as we swooped around the yard like martins.

He had an odd smile, a nearly perfect half-moon, his lips thick at the middle and thin at the ends, that crescent curve, showing no teeth, eyes peeking out from squinted cheeks.

He didn't talk much but he laughed at just about every dumb joke I told and sometimes his laughter was just the thing that got me in trouble, my joke quiet enough to get away with telling it in class but his laugh a perfect arrow that pointed to me. Mrs. Friedman knew, if Jaimie laughed, John David must be the cause. Held after school, just like that.

1854

Our home slowly roused itself, one person at a time. Mama and me tried to find some time to comb out my hair every morning before we prepared breakfast. The boys had rekindled the hearth fire and started another small fire in the kitchen stove and hauled in fresh water and even more wood. I always paused to sort the smells: sulfur and curling wisps of acrid smoke and some mornings chicory coffee, then yeast and breads, meat, and porridge.

My auburn hair was long and kept braided and my secret pride although it wasn't a secret from Mama who privately encouraged— or maybe I should say did not discourage—my long hair since she remembered clearly that as a young woman she had been proud of her long, slightly darker hair, and how she felt when her papa made her cut it when he noticed her extra ministrations. She'd cried it seemed for days, she said, and she didn't want me to feel that loss.

I knew Papa was of two minds about my pride. He encouraged us all to speak our minds, to develop into our own selves. But he also was reserved about some things and I knew he didn't agree with Mama's concerns about my appearance.

I was taller than Mama by nearly a full head, and the same height as Simon but Simon had some growing yet to do. I was solid, a little raw-boned like a boy, and in fact I could run as well as any of the boys and more than one of them found out painfully that I didn't take to gang wrestling any more so they largely left me alone. I'd crossed some divide in the last year or so.

I missed some of the attention but knew enough to keep to myself all the churnings inside me like a burlap bag stuffed with mice. I was a woman though still some on the girl side of that, still eager to run through an island of weeds or throw myself into the swimming hole up around the first bend or giggle at a kitten in a duel with a ball of yarn.

Sometimes I caught Papa looking at me like you'd look at something surprising, like the thing had changed in a blink and what you thought it was it wasn't no more. Mama said he wished I could stay a little girl forever and that my long hair brought both solace and a kind of sadness—each added inch marked another piece of time and then him losing me to some stranger. Mama and I laughed at that though I sensed what brought our smiles was different, that I smiled from the mystery of my unknown future and Mama because of my familiar past.

Back in Tennessee I wouldn't miss school for anything and read books I borrowed from my teacher, Miss Black. Here we had no school yet but I devoured anything on paper and read all the pamphlets and broadsheets that Papa or the older boys brought home from town.

More and more the broadsheets and bills worried over the border raids or the state-supported Southern riff-raff flooding in from Georgia and Tennessee and the Carolinas.

That would be us, which gave me pause, what people would think without the benefit of knowing what kind of people we truly were. There weren't signs posted at our gate announcing Runaway Slaves Un-Welcome, no flags signaling our intentions.

Since Osawatomie was a mere seventeen miles from the Missouri border, much was written about the border ruffians and the midnight murders, ambushes, torched homesteads, destroyed crops, slaughtered livestock, and the wives and daughters that were violated.

Reading the broadsheets was sure to send you to reading the Bible, to balance out the piles of words that filled your head with horrible thoughts. The air itself seemed full to bursting with nervousness and even a bird's shadow was enough to make a grown man wince, his eyes dart from shape to shape, hairs rising on his neck like soldiers on guard duty.

Papa and William and Drury and Simon worked long days, from before the sun came up until it was too dark to see what they were doing, and they mostly finished what I guess you'd call our house after a few weeks. Wasn't anything like our real house back in Tennessee. That was a regular house, wood on all sides, roof, windows, porch, couple rooms and a couple blanket curtains for more rooms.

Here we'd been living in a tent that Papa had rigged up using the wagon as a support, but it was small and either too hot or too cold and didn't offer much protection from things and the wind took it down more than once and we learned right off that storms out on the plains have a lot more spunk than what we'd seen in Tennessee.

They were kind of pretty to see coming at us from the west and southwest, the sky turning a roiling black mess of clouds and an odd yellow band of color between the dark clouds and the horizon, like a piece of the sky ripped away.

We'd been lucky so far, not seeing nor being in no twisters but it was all anyone talked about starting late spring when the days heated up and weather moved through so fast and different you could have every possible thing happen in one day, sunshine, rain, sleet, snow, the whole list. It took my breath away and made me giddy as it seemed God was playing jokes on us, keeping us off-balance.

And it was because of the weather that Papa said we were going to build a house that would be partway in the ground, in the side of a little knoll, we'd have a wood front with two windows and the door, and he promised there'd be a wide porch where Mama and all us could sit and watch the settling west sky. But the back wall and most of the two side walls were dirt with wood walls so it at least looked normal but it was dark and smelled like a hole and that first winter about killed us all as we rode out the big storms; we were warm, I cannot argue with that; the hillside curved around us and held us like pups, the wood stove putting out a lot of heat.

But when we could we were outside, playing in the snow or doing work, hoping to get the land ready, clear more trees and rocks—oh, lord, the rocks, everywhere like scattered beads, but we moved them and used them to make fences and posts. We didn't waste no part of that land, we used what was given us and we used it all and we gave back everything we were, tended it like our lives depended on it.

1954

The statue was life-size and measured five-nine but because it was mounted on a platform of red granite rocks the size of footballs held together by concrete, it loomed over me like the wild-haired, long-bearded wrathful God of the Old Testament.

John Brown's likeness was cast in bronze by the same French foundry that produced the Statue of Liberty. There's a plaque set into the front proclaiming the statue was the gift of the Woman's Relief Corps and that it was dedicated in 1935.

Brown's left leg was bent at the knee, his booted foot slightly ahead of his right, as though caught in mid-step, except his weight was clearly on his back foot: waiting for something that he was more than ready for with his Sharps rifle slung over his right shoulder, his hand holding the sling and his sleeves rolled to his elbows, ready for God's work.

I think it was the rifle, that short carbine, that occupied my imagination and made the statue into something more than it was. I'd been to the art museum in Kansas City and seen rows of gleaming suits of armor, hollow knights with broad swords longer than I was tall, but none of that compared to John Brown, unprotected by anything, but filled out, a solid man and his weapon almost hidden when viewed from the front. But there was more fierceness, more determination, more resolve and danger in that pose, eyes boring into something right there in front of him.

1854

One Saturday early that first spring the sky was dark with crows. You'd have thought a thundercloud chattered overhead, their shadows shifting across the yard like blowing rain.

Papa had promised Simon and I could go into town with him for some flour and molasses and he'd promised Mama she could buy some cotton fabrics for clothes. I hadn't been to town since all the trouble up in Lawrence and I wanted to hear for myself the stories Simon'd been telling me, things he heard from who knows where.

We got up early and did our chores and then washed up and I put on a dress I hadn't worn since last fall that I'd kept tucked away, folded neat and clean. It was tighter than I remembered and a little shorter in the arms, but not so much I considered changing.

Mama made sure we all looked our best and Papa sat quietly out on the wagon while we finished up. Sometimes he was sweet like that to Mama, not saying anything when he could have easily been impatient with our fussiness.

William said he would stay behind and keep an eye on things, and when he said it I saw Mama look at Papa, and Drury and Simon look at William, and they all had the same look, the way you look when you have something down a hole and you're undecided about sticking your hand in there or waiting to see what comes out on its own. I don't think it's something quite like fear but there's a part of it that clearly knows about staying awake and your eye on things.

Going to town back home didn't have all the elevated emotions it did here, or rather, we only trembled with excitement about seeing new things, pretty patterned cotton from New Orleans or some shiny leatherworks that smelled rich as coffee or some kind of traveling show, magic men or dramatic actors or trained animals from Africa.

But here there was all that—well, no trained animals from the dark continent yet—with the added spark of men lounging around with rifles leaned against handy trees or walls, or groups of men and women bunched around a broadsheet tacked up on a building front, big words marching across the top saying how bad things were all around us though especially in Lawrence or up near Westport and St. Joes.

Sometimes two or three men on horses would just thunder down Main Street, sending citizens diving. Once I looked up and saw one of the horsemen riding off, hunched forward over his horse, one arm flailing, urging his horse faster, the other clutching the reins, rifle stock flapping against the horse's shoulder, his handsome face alight with something I almost felt embarrassed to witness.

He was a lone rider, none others in sight and I have no idea why he was pushing that horse the way he was but the pounding hooves and billowing dust and the rider's urgency took my breath away.

Every voice, every posted broadside seemed to swell the air with its own importance and the noise of it became the backdrop of our visits to town.

The boys—William and Drury and Simon even—huddled together at the drop of a hat talking about the war swirling around us, the rights of some men over some other men was how it was, they all agreed no white man should be a slave to no one, but only Simon sometimes said maybe no man should own another, no matter the other is a nigger, no matter the other is anything, but he was too young and outnumbered and they shut him up or sent him away and since they were who he wanted to be with, the older brothers, he shut his mouth or said the right things and they continued to plot actions against the numerous foes they perceived lurking just beyond our sight. They imagined nightriders over the last rise, in the gully, holding burning torches in one hand, Sharps rifles in the other, the reins of their fire-breathing horses in their teeth, their eyes bright glowing coals.

How it seemed to me, them boys playing soldier games, thinking they could plug themselves into the real-life war that was truly roaring around us. It was a fact you could hear rifle shots in the middle of the night. And the wind could bring the sound of horses thundering nearby, and you could see men argue and push each other on Main Street in town.

Hardly anything you could imagine was a stretch to imagine as true—what men did to each other in anger or righteousness was not beyond our worst imaginings. There wasn't anything we couldn't do to each other, that seemed clear and something I believe everyone knows in their hearts, knows is there, something compressed and black, the size of a pea; it is the dark dark knowledge that cruelty lives in us, something we all get as part of our humanity, an inherited thing that jerks you awake at night, that hears things you didn't know you heard, that registers some off-kilter angle of the light as danger, that rules your will when you are cornered and bloodied. This thing is the root of every murder we do in the name of something else. Higher callings are the hooks we hang our fears and anger on, if you ask me.

1954

Each school year some fad or two swept through the grades like a flu bug. This year's first was marbles.

One before had been whirligigs that we bought at Fat's, the little grocery store across the street from Meek. I don't remember the store's real name, but everyone called it Fat's because the man who ran it was huge. He sold penny candy and in the spring baseball cards with those chalky-white-pink slabs of gum inside. And cheap toys: the whirligigs, which were brightly colored propellers atop a six-inch stick that you held between your palms and then rapidly set into flight by just rubbing your palms past each other.

Marbles were played for keeps, most games, and it was a serious decision putting your best cleary or cat's-eye on the line. Some kids showed up with steelies, which were prized since they were heavy and shined and made a great clunk sound.

The steelies were in fact ball bearings and the kids who had them got them from their daddies who brought them home from the Union Pacific. Bombers was called when you wanted to stand over your opponent's marble and drop yours like a bomb. It wasn't that easy to hit anything—although you'd squint real hard—but when a steelie hit a glass marble, serious damage almost always resulted, which, I guess, made Bombers more an act of meanness than good gamesmanship since the victor often got nothing for his skill other than a handful of splintered glass. It also made winning back your marble a moot point.

We gathered on the east side of school not too far from the main doorway. An area of dirt about ten feet on each side had been cleared of rocks and sticks and other debris, including the shiny black chunks of coal that littered the schoolyard. The twins, Woody, and I set up for a game when the Catholic kid came over.

I'm in this too, he said.

Woody and I looked at each other, blank faces, each hoping the other would say something. No soap. The twins murmured something and Brad said they wanted to shoot somewhere else and they left.

I'd just the day before won a beautiful cleary, which instantly became my most prized marble. It had been the first time I'd allowed myself to be talked into playing for keeps and I'd won, which went a long way toward undermining my fear of losing my possessions. Still, now that I'd won, I didn't much want to lose it back and so I elected to play with another favorite, another slightly larger than normal shooter, this one a smoky blue.

I don't want that one, said the Catholic kid. His face set into a scowl, which it was pretty much all the time. I want your cleary.

He'd seen me win the day before and had tried to get me to play him then. In fact, he'd been in line to play against the kid I'd won it from so in his mind it was his prize deferred.

I don't want to play with that one, I said.

Then you can't play, he said. Right, Woody?

Woody shrugged. What did he care? It wasn't his marble up for grabs.

I don't know why, but for some reason I felt I didn't have any choice, that simply walking away wasn't an option. But I didn't want to lose my new favorite.

I'm gonna play with my blue shooter, I said. You can go play somewhere else, you want.

What'd you say? said the Catholic kid, moving a foot closer to me.

I backed away before I had a chance to even think of standing up to him.

I don't want to use my cleary, I said.

Tough shit, he said. You afraid of losing?

None of us swore. He could get away with anything.

No, I said, though I was afraid of losing or getting beat up if I didn't play.

Then play, he said. He couldn't be bluffed since he called everything. I hated being the chicken to the Catholic kid's bully act. He'd had my number since school started.

Okay, I said.

I had been playing my heart out that week, been shooting marbles dead-on from across ten feet of rocky, cinder-littered school yard, but I just didn't like chancing my new cleary. I wanted it. I felt cornered, my choices taken away by my fear of getting into a fight I was sure I'd lose.

The Catholic kid went first and he surprised no one by standing over the playing circle, his steelie held between his thumb and first finger, one eye closed, aiming his bomber.

He opened the closed eye and turned his head and gave me a look, said, I'm gonna smash your cleary to pieces, and then he swiveled his head back, shut his eye again, and opened his fingers, the shiny steel ball bearing plopping into the cinders about a half inch from my cleary.

He kicked at the ground, sent up a small black cloud and stepped away.

Things sometimes turn out in your favor. I kneeled down and carefully lined up my shooting hand and shot, popping the Catholic kid's steelie.

Bingo, the game was over and maybe that helped get me out of it in one piece since it was too sudden for the Catholic kid to work himself into a fit over the loss of his shooter.

He glared at me for a full minute and then walked away. The whole time he stared at me my head was jammed with thoughts, what to do if he jumped me, where I could run, what I'd yell, hoping to draw help. I was miserable, being so much a chicken.

And when he turned and stalked off, leaving his marble in the circle for me to collect, I didn't quite believe it, expected him to spin around and charge, tackle me, wrestle me to the ground, wail on me with his fists. But he kept walking away. You could just about see him twitching.

I couldn't help it, I broke into a grin, maybe even giggled. Woody looked as startled as I felt.

It sealed our fate, the Catholic kid and me.

1960

John David

We sat there and drank for who knows how long, maybe an hour, hard to keep track, the place so dark, everything about it timeless and slowed down, like you could walk in there and not leave for a couple years and it would seem like fifteen minutes. When later I had to go to the bathroom, I looked the place over better, saw that a ton of sadness had visited this place, plain moved in and thrown a party, and the other drinkers looked like they'd received the invite and resigned themselves willingly to all its quiet sorrow.

Starting out, Dorthea did most of the talking, about her baby brother, Delbert, how he was always in some kind of scrape, but a good boy at heart. I told her about my little brother, who was never in trouble but sure ought to be, the stuff he got away with. Woody mostly listened and sucked on his drink. He seemed to sink lower with each sip. It was like watching the sun slide into the fields.

Every few minutes she touched my leg, little pats or sometimes a fast rub, like she was trying to bring herself some good luck. Each time was sudden, like I'd backed into one of those electric wires my granddad used to keep the cats out of his garden, jolting me like I'd been asleep when I'd already been pretty wide awake, that kind of startling contrast.

Looking back, I should have noticed how Woody wasn't having quite the same good time I was, how he was in fact brooding, and I had only thought him listening, without much to say.

Where you boys off to next, she asked, her eyes flicking from Woody to me.

Hadn't thought much about it, I said. Our plans seem to have changed. I smiled for her, a little nod.

Got to go home sometime, said Woody, Osawatomie, barely loud enough to be heard.

They kick you outta here at one, and I'm just getting started, she said.

She grinned big, eyes flaring.

Could go with you, she said, soft like.

It ain't anywhere near here, said Woody, his voice sounding peevish, as though telling the truth would ruin everything.

Well, I don't care about that, she said. Let's just go and worry about all that later. Come on.

I don't know, Woody said, shaking his head. There ain't nothing to do. He looked at me. That's why we came up here, he said.

He's right, I said. It's getting pretty late.

I ain't never been to Aus-a-wot-o-me, she said, drawing out the name, saying it wrong like most everyone else, that big white smile ricocheting from me to Woody.

That's Oh-sa-wa-toe-me, said Woody, real slow, a English lesson. Say it right.

She dropped her smile just that fast.

What's going on here, she said, not so much angry as surprised. What's you doing?

Showing you how to say our town, said Woody.

She looked at him, not talking, I think trying to decide how serious he was or how serious she was gonna be or both.

People sometimes make fun of it, I said, so we're, you know, a little touchy about it, that's all. He doesn't mean nothing more than that, right, Woody?

Woody looked at me.

Yeah, I guess, he said.

Well, hell, she said, her smile taking over again, let's go, show me this fine place. You know, she said, remembering, it seemed like, I think there's someone down there owes my brother some money. I could get it for him, bail him out of jail, her voice all hopeful and girly.

Woody and I looked at each other, the complications stacking up like a kid's wood blocks, getting too high, waiting to tumble over.

I dunno, said Woody. That don't concern us much.

Oh, I know that, she said. You just take me there, I can do the rest, eyes pinballing.

Something dull and serious hung over the booth, weighing us down, killing our high time. I sensed things shifting, all the earlier burlesque energy slipping into some future nervous event.

It'd be a big help, she said.

Up to Woody, I said. It's his car.

Woody's look said it all: thanks a big heap.

Come on, Woody, she said. We'll have some fun and I'll get my brother's money and then you can come back up some other night. You'll be my personal heroes. Beaming at us like we were children waiting in line at the Sears and Roebuck for Santa Claus.

Woody's head dipped, like some muscle gave out, and that's all the signal she needed. She started pushing against me, moving me out of the booth. I paid Archie, who didn't say a thing, and we left.

1854

O ur farm took most of our time. We had fields to clear and turn over and plant and tend. Some fences to string across a few acres of slightly rolling prairie; outbuildings and a well—and a fine log portal through which every visitor had to ride. Papa and Mama said they'd been talking and knew what they wanted the farm to be called and we all thought it was good so the next day the boys went out and found some tall, straight pine trees, felled them and trimmed them and hawed them and put them together and me and Simon painted the name on some pieces of wood the boys had attached to a frame, the sign three feet tall and eight feet wide and in thick black carefully hand-painted letters the name, Dawson.

I used to lie in the tall grass just south of the little knoll that rose like a grave between where I was and the house, lie there on those steamy summer days and watch the chicken hawks and red tails and big black crows turn in the hot air, rising like spirits up into heaven. The crows—as big as chickens—slicing across the sky before darting into tree tops where they called out to anything that'd listen to their chatter. I know the hawks capture everyone's mind with their soaring and all that gliding on those big wide wings, but I must admit I loved the crows most, something about their haughty airs and the way they had nothing to do but scatter the other birds or play with rocks or twigs, and I'd see myself one of them, coasting on some hot air over our farm or over the big lookout mound or the Doumas, the Adairs, or even as far as Osawatomie, and I'd see things I knew I had no business knowing, things that I later learned were true and factual.

I flew in the afternoon heat or with the morning's first red light or even at night, my wings flapping out the window and up, up, up over the first trees, following the twinkling lights overhead.

I could see everything.

1954

During most of that year I had a crush on Sharon Marie. It wasn't something I thought about or talked about with anyone; I didn't even think about it as a crush. I just became aware that I liked her a lot and that I looked forward to talking to her. It excited me to think what the others might say if they knew or if I said something to Sharon Marie and we learned we were thinking the same thing.

Her skin looked like polished dark wood and her eyes were big and she always seemed happy to see me. I liked her. And I had no idea what to do about it, knowing, somehow, that I'd cross some kind of line if I admitted to myself she was my girlfriend or that I could feel that way about her; it felt like if I did such a thing, I'd get in trouble, and that both frightened me and thrilled me, made my heart flutter, my stomach ache whenever I thought about her or was with her. She was forbidden and I couldn't quite understand that, why that was so or what it meant.

You bring your lunch today, John David, she asked soon as Mrs. Friedman had let us loose.

Yeah, thinking about what Mama had said this morning. Peanut butter and jelly and an apple. I could feel the apple through the paper bag.

I got baloney, she said, just the hint of a giggle following.

We went down the street to the high school and climbed to the third floor hallway and had lunch in one corner and talked and watched the high school kids take up the hall with a noon dance, a 45 record player going at the other end, music echoing off the hard floor and steel lockers, the polished floor shimmering with bob-by-soxed feet.

I stared at the older kids, how pretty some of the colored girls looked.

I pointed at one, said, she sure is pretty. Is that Diane's sister? It seemed safe to say something like that about a senior, about someone's sister. It was almost like saying something about a grownup.

Sharon Marie nodded her head, watched.

It wasn't the first time we'd talked about the older girls and how pretty they were, and every time we had those talks I felt like I was in truth talking about her and that what I was really saying was how pretty she was but I couldn't say that out loud, not to her face, so instead I said that about the dancers, like they were some ideal and Sharon Marie'd be like them when she got a little older, that I was saying someday we could maybe dance during the noon hour, instead of us just watching.

I wish I could dance like that, she said.

What they were doing looked almost impossible, spinning and hopping and sliding across the floor, waving their arms, and everyone smiling and laughing. It was something I could never do.

It looks too hard, I said.

She glanced at me, then back to the action.

I bet you could do it, if you practiced, she said.

I'd have to practice in secret, I said. I'd look like a spastic trying to learn that stuff.

We could do that, she said, her voice low. I bet we could learn it together, surprise everyone someday, get up there and dance our hearts out.

A bubble of something halfway between being a word and being an action ballooned in my chest. I knew the feeling, knew it preceded the loss of all ability to talk and that even now my face was filling up.

Sharon Marie's eyes grew, her face registered concern, puzzlement, then, as things added up, disappointment.

You don't wanna dance with me, she said quietly.

I looked away, the bubble expanded, pressed into my heart, pushed into my lungs, my breath caught.

I just wouldn't be any good, I said. If I could dance I'd dance with you.

Now you're just saying that, she said, taking a peek at the inside of her sandwich, making sure the baloney was still there.

I knew what was going on, in me, I mean. I knew that I was cornered and that if I didn't dance with Sharon Marie, or learn to dance with her, off in secret somewhere, it was dawning on me I'd lose something I didn't want to lose.

My mind latched onto the potential of secret lessons and I started spinning wool, the two of us sneaking around, an authentic illicit relationship—and I had no idea what that meant, did not in truth really know the facts of life, had a vague notion gathered from partially overheard snippets of jokes or comments by teenagers.

And then my alarm when I became aware I had a stiffy.

My face turned darker, breaking fresh ground in areas of red.

Her brows knitted, concerned, her head tilted, lips pursed like she was about to say a word starting with W.

I'll be right back, I said, jumping up, jamming my hands into my pockets as I twisted around so that I was turned away from her and walking toward the bathrooms just down the hall.

I stayed in the bathroom until the stiffy went away, watching my watch, rehearsing my excuses, practicing what I'd say about the other, about dancing, first pretending to be on the toilet, taking up a stall, grunting, then later combing my hair or washing my hands, doing it all over again, peeking at my watch, checking my pants, see if I was sticking out, trying not to think about Sharon Marie and doing nothing but thinking about Sharon Marie.

The stiffy hung in there for twenty-three minutes. When I returned to our corner of the hall, she was gone, just some crumbs there.

1854

Papa and Mama hardly ever preached religion at us. The Bible was handy and we all read from it because it was the only thing to read most times, but Papa said he wanted us to find our own beliefs, we had that right, we had that responsibility. They pointed us in their own direction sure enough but let us figure out our own solutions.

I was smart enough to know we were unusual, impossible not to hear what others said, calling on God to smite one person or another or a state or a part of the country or a whole people. I heard things coming out of children's mouths that I know they had no idea what they were saying, just something they heard their daddies or mamas or big brothers say, angry things that made them think they were then grown up because anger spoken in sentences was listened to and valued and made you important.

If I said anything about this to friends, they made disapproving faces and some stopped talking to me for a while, until the effect wore off or they forgot, I guess. They pretended outrage but you could tell it was just words and they had no inkling about what they believed. What I said confused them with choices where none were supposed to be.

Papa didn't believe in religions, said they were just dull, solemn clubs for lazy bones. Said each man and woman must find God, it wasn't something someone could lead you to. Said it's something you have to do for yourself for it to mean anything. It isn't something you pick up in town shopping. Papa said it's like reading signs, figuring out what's right in front of us.

The Bible ain't itself a religion, he said. It's just good stories about how to live and words to live by. Some are impossible to understand today but Papa says there'd be no way he could explain a steam engine to an ancient, so he figured it went both ways, there's things today the Bible can't address, except in parables but Papa says every darnation thing can be reduced to parable so that doesn't hardly count in a serious argument.

I was unclear how could there be sin if you didn't have religion. And if there isn't any sin is there no right or wrong? It seems they could be separate things, in a world of their own apart from a world that creates religions out of need or fear or boredom, some deeper world where in fact there is less gray and more black and white, a thing done cannot be undone or forgotten, in the natural world one thing eats another, in fact or in a manner of speaking and we don't bother ourselves with words like justice.

I cannot think of a single thing that under some circumstances isn't sanctioned, the state kills murderers and thieves, a king can possess all he covets, and bad men everywhere seem to thrive more often than not.

Some kind of war had been declared or almost so. There were stories of two different territorial governments going at once, free-staters in Shawnee Mission or Lecompton—depended upon who told the story—and the pro-slavers that took over Leavenworth and started the Law and Order Party. Militias popped up like weeds, some nothing more than drunken thugs hanging their hats on Kansas's troubles so they could justify their crimes. You heard about people starting out from someplace and never showing up, later someone volunteered they heard about or saw ruffians or someone's militia.

I had seen some militia, although I wasn't supposed to be anywhere near where I was, so I didn't say anything to Papa or even Simon. There were other reasons, too.

It was early our first fall when I saw a flock of crows rise up like a black sheet from a flaming oak, folding across the bright blue sky, drawing my eyes toward a shimmer, a wrinkle in the air just above the horizon, east.

I watched the liquid air gather its colors and shapes and over time make a collection of men on horses, coming along at a steady but not hurried pace.

I was up a tree, for another purpose altogether, or mostly so, and by the time I recognized what was coming down the roadway, it was too late for me to climb down and get to cover. This part of the road was out in the open, relatively. No other trees nearby large enough to hide behind or in, no large bushes or boulders, and the ravine that wound away from the roadway was too far to make without getting caught out in the open.

I was stuck. I took what little time I had to position myself behind the thickest branch, tried to put it between me and the passing men, now no further than a hundred feet. The entrancing sound of hooves on the hard dirt, a voice, maybe two, chattering about something, sounding about half asleep, like they were out picking apples on Sunday back home and the worst thing that could happen would be to wander into an angry bee.

I made myself stare up into the sky, deflect any look that glanced my way, give them the ribbon of crows to follow.

Creaking leather and the horses' breathing, the steady thump thump ka-thump, and then the odors of the horses and smoke and the bodies of worked-out men, my nose stinging from the sudden storm of dust.

I was dead certain a sneeze I could not stop was building inside my head, like a sharp light growing out of my head, growing too fast to be measured.

I slapped one hand over my face and bit down on my lips and my whole body wracked as the sneeze was blown back inside, just like a little bomb had gone off inside my stomach the way I bounced on that limb and made a sound like a soft melon hitting the side of a big oak.

All the rhythms changed in a beat, the horses drawn up, the leather slapping straight, the voices, more of them, no longer sleepy or quiet, every word ending with a question mark. What? Where? See? Look! And then, you! And I was caught.

That ain't no one, you jackass, another said, slapping his thigh with his hat, laughter rolling out of him. That's just an ol' crow. You done spooked yourself, Ike.

The one had yelled at me angled his head, trying to see past the leaves and branches. I angled mine, mirrored him, my black eye winking.

It was a hard summer. Storms rolled over us like runaway boulders, wind like I never could have imagined, grown trees danced across the prairie and our fields—it'd fool you, thinking that's a little branch flying by right in front of you except it was a whole giant oak tree a couple hundred feet away. Papa had been smart and dug our house so most of the southwest portion was the part in the dirt and all these trees and brush hopped on over us, though we did lose a horse, its neck broken by something that roared through one dark night.

All of us worked the ground, turning rugged prairie into fields, hauling out enough rock to build a shelter for the animals and start a good fence; and trees and their stumps, burnt down to black lumps we spread into the dirt.

We had one good plow animal and William and Drury or sometimes one of them and Simon would wrap a harness over their shoulders, two at a time, and they'd pull a till around that me or Simon would guide and we cut deep furrows and then Mama dropped seeds and covered them up, and then after we'd all help carry buckets of water and dribble them empty where we dropped seeds and then we gathered and prayed for rain and sunshine and kind winds.

We got it all, and more. We had the good weather but we also had the bad, winds and hard hard rains and then heat or late cold, something. We had the kind of success that got us along but not the kind that let us rest. The work just never seemed to stop.

Still, Papa said it could've been a lot worse. We had corn and potatoes and turnips and cabbage and even beans, enough he believed, to get us through. And there was still a chance the late grain might come in big enough we could trade for another horse since we were one down.

Mama asked for my help sorting through the boys' clothes, in hopes, she said, of finding enough outgrown or worn-out things to allow her to start a winter patch quilt. I knew as well as she did how thin things were so I did not harbor any sentiment we would be as successful as she wanted, and true enough, even though we tried to condemn pairs of trousers and cotton shirts, we knew we needed all we had just to keep us warm over the coming winter.

Her eyes looked as dry and red as wilted oak leaves and I dared not let my gaze linger or else its heat inflame her humors. I was shamed by my own embarrassment for her and for what we did not have.

Leaving Tennessee had been as painful as forcing a child to give away a litter of favorite kittens, the one salve that our new life on the frontier would redeem every sacrifice, but now, after only a year and a month, it began to seem as though the problem was not where we were but that we were.

The Dawsons were as likely to fail in Kansas as Tennessee or anywhere else. It was the kind of thinking that could drag you down and fulfill its promise. It had a weight you felt in your knees and back and neck. It was as real as the exhaustion you felt sometimes when you opened your eyes after a fitful night of dreams you couldn't remember but knew you'd had and wished you hadn't.

I told her to go ahead and start dinner—I'd be along shortly—and I'd take care of putting the old clothes back in their places. She simply nodded and then stood and shuffled off toward the stores where she picked through the potatoes and carrots and onions until she found just the ones she wanted.

1954

The Catholic kid had been in and out of our classes from kindergarten on. Word had it he was in the Catholic school when he wasn't in ours. Or some kind of trouble. No one really knew for sure, it was all just talk, him showing up one year, or some part of a year. Then gone, the same way. I couldn't think of anyone who liked him.

And you'd hear things, when he got in trouble for carrying knives or breaking a store window or pulling down stop signs or taking away the ruler a nun had been using on him and giving her a few whacks. He was notorious and he was our age. He was the kind of kid who truly scared grownups.

No one wanted to sit next to the Catholic kid. He dressed funny. He wore thick, wrinkled flannel shirts, today's version a dull red, crowded with little black cowboys and Indians and bucking horses, twisted, twirling lariats. All the buttons that could button were buttoned and his freckled red face looked squeezed out of his shirt; his red hair was thick and clumpy and somehow added to his mean looks although I suppose it was his dark blue eyes and the way they hid back under his thick brow like electric charges that really made him seem so mean.

The weirdest smell rose from his shirt, some chemical odor that I instinctively knew wasn't right. I couldn't stand it. How could anyone wear something that smelled that bad?

Mrs. Friedman called me to the blackboard to divide some numbers, a cinch, but I had to walk by the Catholic kid so I took a big breath and held it until I was all the way up front and then I let it out and breathed normal again.

Jaimie, who sat across the aisle from the Catholic kid, giggled. He was leaning dangerously out into the opposite aisle, trying to get as far away from the Catholic kid as he could and the giggling must have tipped his balance because next thing he started to fall into the aisle except that he caught himself with his other arm but not before Mrs. Friedman saw him and gave him one of those frozen-in-time stares, bright red lips pressed together and her chin tucked in all serious, eyes aimed at you like a firing squad. And tapping her leg with a ruler. I think that was the part that scared me the most, that tapping, rat-a-tat-tat, and if you were the guy and she tapped and tapped and walked closer there was always that chance she might suddenly rap-a-tat-rap on your head with that ruler. We'd all seen it done and I'd got it once already.

Jaimie pulled himself together and kept his eyes focused on something on his desktop and Mrs. Friedman tapped but did not move and I felt better because I knew it was my holding my breath that made Jaimie giggle.

I turned to the blackboard and did the long division, took forty-seven into three-hundred-and-ninety-two.

Is that right, Mrs. Friedman? I said. She had green eyes and a triangular face, her chin the point.

She finished tapping and looked at me, just looked at me, and then her eyes flared and she looked at the board, worked through my arithmetic, and said it was fine. Then she told me to take my seat and she watched me the whole way back plus she was standing toward the back so I was walking right toward her so I did not hold my breath with my cheeks all puffed out or anything, just walked by the Catholic kid as fast as I could, but I must have done something, grimaced or made a face or something because Mrs. Friedman slapped the ruler against her leg, made a big loud slap and everyone froze including me.

What was that, John David?

What, I said. What was what?

I really didn't know. I'd hurried by but I hadn't consciously done anything, made a face or held my nose or anything like that.

You know what I mean, she said.

I just wanted to get back to my seat, I said, hoping that it was just my speedy retreat that had gotten her attention.

I don't think that's the truth, she said. Her mouth was straight and tight and her eyes blazed into mine. I'm waiting, John David, she said.

I was just trying to get by, that's all, I said.

Was he doing something to you? she said.

No.

Then what do you mean you had to get by him? Why?

I could feel things coming in on me, the air darkening, shrinking light, a sense of something almost thick between me and everything going on in the room. Except I could hear the Catholic kid's breathing, heavier, deeper than the others', growing into a growl.

His shirt, I said, hoping that that was enough. I couldn't be the only one who thought his shirt smelled funny.

What about his shirt, John David? Was it bothering you?

Jaimie giggled. Someone else did too, over on the side next to the windows. A girl, probably Martha. I glanced at Lonnie and saw him roll his eyes.

It smells, I said. And frightened as I was I surprised myself with a bubble of noise that I couldn't repress. A few others answered.

Mrs. Friedman silenced the room with a tight-lipped glare that flowed from window row to far wall row. Eyes dropped to the floor almost in unison; you could, I swear, hear it, a quick clicking like the last rustling of an injured bird.

Mrs. Friedman was quiet. I guess she didn't think I'd say that.

What do you mean? Her voice had lost most of its hardness. Maybe I had a point.

It smells funny, I said.

Your face smells funny.

I wheeled around to see the Catholic kid leaning forward out of his desk, one hand gripping the desk, the other the back of his seat. He was growling again.

Look, I'm sorry, I said. Your shirt's fine. It was just a joke.

The growling grew louder. His desk started to rattle and the kid behind him, Woody, sat on the far edge of his seat, away from the action.

The Catholic kid added a nasty gurgle to the growl. He sounded just like the bulldog that sometimes charged me inside its fenced-in yard, the dog snarling and growling and bouncing off the fencing until I left its sidewalk territory.

Mrs. Friedman called out the Catholic kid's name, commanded him to sit still as she strode over to our aisle.

The Catholic kid continued to growl but his intensity had been broken, her shout distracting him.

Turn around in that seat. Right now.

The Catholic kid returned his gaze to me. It looked like his entire face was rippling and his eyes were as big as egg yolks.

I'm gonna get you, he whispered just before he swiveled around and faced the blackboard.

Mrs. Friedman walked up our row and stood over me. My eyes were focused on my desktop. My head felt hot. There wasn't much to look at on my desk.

You stay for recess, she said.

She turned and continued toward the front, past the Catholic kid. She slowed a little right before she reached him and seemed to look around the room there, her eyes darting briefly toward the Catholic kid, then away, and she finished the trip back to her desk where she pivoted and sat down and looked out the window.

At recess I stayed in my desk while everyone else stood and hurried out, no one wanting to waste a minute. Sharon Marie offered me a shy smile when she went by. I smiled back, followed her with my eyes.

John David, said Mrs. Friedman. I want your attention up here.

Yes ma'am, I said. My hands were joined atop my desk, my back stiff.

She asked me why I couldn't get along with the Catholic kid. I said there was no reason and I would try better and I was sorry I caused any trouble. It came out in a tumble, like I'd tripped and spilled the words.

She sat and looked at me, her mouth a little unsteady, either about to say something or resisting the words, then she went still and her eyes cut to whatever was going on out the wall of windows, in the trees. We were on the top floor.

She looked back at me. Okay, she said. I'll expect that from you, you two get along. Now go on, join the others, you've got ten minutes.

School was okay the rest of the day, the regular stuff. Someone threw an eraser, a bunch of notes, folded up in elaborate ways, were passed, mostly by the girls, although Woody almost got caught, got away with it by eating it real fast, which made him break into a fit of giggles, which he then could not explain, Mrs. Friedman turning a red to match her hair. Sometimes we drove her nuts, you could tell.

I kept trying to catch Sharon Marie's eye but where she sat and where I sat made it hard, and I was trying to do it without alerting anyone else, wanting to keep it between us two. I mean, I hardly talked to or let on I knew any of the girls, white or colored, and Sharon Marie being colored made it even harder.

Every time I felt I could look back and over toward the windows, where she sat, she had her head down, her pencil in her hand, her face a mask of concentration, doing problems or copying spelling words.

A few weeks back, after I'd been a smart aleck, I guess, Mrs. Friedman made me teach arithmetic after we came in from recess. She sat at my desk and drummed on the top with her fingers and pencil, just like I did. I was flustered and my lesson kind of dragged out. Some of the kids gave me a hard time. Teacher's-pet stuff and regular you're-a-jerk stuff and he's-spoiled stuff, real dislike, I guess. I remember I looked at Mrs. Friedman toward the end when nothing I said made anyone stop saying things or giggling and I was ready to sit down, I was getting filled up with something. Her eyes were red, like she'd had something in there and rubbed too hard. She let me sit down. After that I'd been trying to be a little quieter.

I guess that hadn't worked too well. I felt bad, making Mrs. Friedman unhappy.

Jaimie came to school one day, eyes heavy, mouth pulled down, no smile of any kind.

I asked him what was going on.

Nothing.

You in trouble? Do something?

I said I can't talk about it.

I stared at him, his face defiant now, but also wanting me to drop it. I was making it hard on him. I told him everything, just plain everything.

Later, back in class Martha kept giving me this weird smile, like she had a secret and if I just said the right thing or looked at her right, she'd be happy to tell me, my reward for falling into the trap.

At recess, the one before lunch, she came up to me, that silly smile leading the way.

I know something you don't know, she said, eyes glinting light.

Anything you know I don't isn't anything I'd want to know anyway, I said.

I know something about Jaimie you don't, she said, her face a little darker, her eyes lowered a bit, letting me in on things. Being serious, generous.

This surprised me. None of the girls hardly paid any attention to any of the colored boys. I could sense my face going through a ripple of confusion.

You don't even talk to Jaimie, I said.

Dummy, I don't have to talk to him to know something about him, she said, her grin reflecting her scored point.

You don't know anything, I repeated.

It's a secret, she half whispered, leaning toward me a few inches. I leaned back, couldn't help myself. I looked around quickly, hoped no one was watching. We were talking too long. Martha's shadow Gail was hovering.

I'm gonna tell you, she said, moving a little closer, leaning toward my ear.

I couldn't help it, I turned my ear toward her.

Two things happened: She whispered, His daddy's in jail. And as soon as she said it, as fast as you could think it, she kissed me twice on the cheek, and then ran away, laughing, Gail at her side, also laughing, both of them glancing back at me.

I felt my face go hot. I looked around again, checking for witnesses, saw Jaimie over by a tree, happening to be looking my way, I thought, his face as down as it had looked this morning. As soon as he noticed I saw him he looked away, out toward the street, where a car was going slowly by. A black and white city police car, its uniformed driver gazing our way, his eyes lingering on us or maybe just Jaimie standing alone near the tree.

I walked over to where he was. Jaimie, I said, talk to me.

He gave me a look.

Come on, I said.

Ain't got nothing to do with you. Family stuff, he said.

I know, I said.

He looked at me like I'd just walked into the room, like he'd turned around and seen me there, one minute I wasn't there, next minute I was.

What do you think you know?

Martha said your daddy was in jail, I said, quietly, leaning toward him. His eyes were dark and round and shined in the light. He turned his head, looked at the ground, kicked at the cinders.

This ain't got nothing to do with nothing, he said. And it sure ain't got nothing to do with you.

I'm your friend, aren't I?

He met my eyes, his dark pools that opened up like holes into a place that had no bottom, like a well you drop a stone into, it'd just fall and fall and fall and you'd never hear nothing. He blinked.

Yeah, you're my friend, he said. But my daddy ain't done nothing wrong and I don't want nobody talking about it.

I nodded and he nodded back and then he smiled his shy smile, dipped his head, and I thought to myself, we're okay.

Jaimie's daddy, like just about everyone else, worked for the railroad, at the roundhouse. Biggest repair yard west of the Mississippi. Every school kid got at least one tour of the roundhouse, got to climb around a switch engine, and was given, if the class was really lucky, handfuls of ball bearings gleaming so bright it looked like a fist of light.

Jaimie's daddy did something down in the pit, under the engines, came out covered by a thick layer of black grease, this large colored man, took him almost an hour to clean up after he came home, running through two tanks of hot water, Jaimie's daddy sitting on the closed toilet seat, reading a book while the hot-water heater did its job. Went through soap like ice cream.

This is just the stuff I knew from Jaimie, from things all year long at school. It wasn't like we talked about our daddies and mamas, except he'd said his daddy was fast, like him, had been a star in school, and I told about my daddy lettering in three sports and almost breaking the state half-mile mark. Not a thought came to mind about why Jaimie's daddy would be in jail.

Not that day, nor even the next, but after a couple days I asked Mama about Jaimie's daddy, getting around to the jail part toward the end. Had she heard anything?

She looked at me like she looked at Larry when he said some of the things he said.

Where'd you hear that? she wanted to know. Her face was drawn up tight, and I didn't know what I'd done to get in this much trouble.

Martha, I said. Martha's daddy knew everything. He owned the Texaco station on Main Street just east of the tracks. Howie's. Everyone knew that all truly useful information channeled through there. It's where the weekly newspaper pointed its reporters when they'd heard about something but didn't know who to ask to learn more; someone at Howie's would know something.

Well, I haven't heard a word, she said.

Smiles weren't intended to look brittle so what I got was more severe than that. I don't think that until that moment my Mama ever considered that anything more than Disney cartoons ran unending in my head, and here she found out her son played with colored children and knew one well enough to wonder about his jailbird daddy.

1960

Woody

It was John David's idea, the whole shebang. Going up to the city, seeing the burlesque. And then this nigger girl came along and for some damn reason John David let her take us into that bar, where we had no business in the first place, none of us twenty-one and this being Missouri.

I just don't know why I let him talk me into things all the time. It's my damn car, too. Sweet fifty-three Buick Super, the two-door hardtop model, white with a red roof. A new custom red Lucite gearshift knob I put on barely two weeks ago. Baby Moon hubs over black wheels and white sidewalls. A true beauty.

Earlier on the way out of town we stopped at Howie's, on Main just east of the tracks. You drove your car under a solid brick roof that stuck out from the red brick building, all painted Texaco red. Howie and his help all wore khaki green uniforms with the solid-billed policeman's hats with the red star on the crown. Looked just like the guys on Milton Berle.

He said he'd get the gas, paid for a whole tank of ethyl, a big grin for Howie who himself wiped off the windshield and asked if he could check the oil, the tires. John David waved him off, still grinning like one of them nuts out at the state hospital. This was my car, remember, him acting like it's his, even Howie acting like it's his, taking his money, saying how nice it looked, and me there behind the wheel, some kind of invisible chauffeur, I guess.

I drove up U.S. 50 and John David fiddled with the radio, punching one button after another, looking, he said, for some jumping music. He settled on WHB and then sat there, bobbing his head, snapping his fingers, grinning that grin out at no one except maybe the cows.

We made a quick stop in Paola at a little grocery store for an eight-pack of Coors Banquets. John David used the church key I kept in the glove box to open us each a beer and we settled back for the trip. I felt better, the beer in my hand, the other guiding the big Buick. The music John David found wasn't so bad. Maybe they'd play "Honky Tonk."

John David used to be more fun, back in grade school. Maybe things were just funner then. Certainly weren't no niggers marching in the streets or Catholics running for president, holy Christ that one caught me by surprise.

Things wasn't like they used to be and I thought they was just fine before. It's the before part I get confused because I can't look back and point at any one thing that started things to go bad.

Not like John David. He can look back to the exact day his luck turned on him although he acts like he's all recovered and his life is a basket of peaches. Maybe that's why he struts around my car or any damn thing—acting like the world is his when everyone knows different.

I always got a little turned around in the city but we found Twelfth Street and then the burlesque and then, a few minutes later, a place to park the car that seemed okay. Not a whole lot of people out but enough and not all of them were niggers so I thought the car'd be there when we got back.

The couple beers I had, I was ready to charge on to the show, see my first pair of naked titties, but John David stopped me and said we needed a story, since we were not twenty-one and they might ask us about that.

I don't think they care a whole lot, John David, I said, darting my eyes toward the rows of winking white lights wrapped around the front of the theater like a pair of pale arms. Bobby and Dwight and Johnny Bob didn't have no trouble couple weeks ago and I know we look older than them boys. It was their stories that got us wound up and led to us standing there on the sidewalk, a mere half-block away. I could almost see those girls through the brick wall, I was so ready for it.

Let's just go, I said.

I think we need to have something ready to say, so we don't get caught off-guard, start chattering like a park squirrel, give ourselves away, he said. His voice has this way of sounding like a teacher's sometimes and it can drive you crazy, like it was then.

If we act like we're twenty-one, we'll be twenty-one, I said, liking the ring of it.

He looked at me, that patient give-it-a-second-thought look, like some grade school teacher. I'm sure that's where he picked it up, back in school.

Which was when the nigger girl came from out of nowhere, and next thing I knew everything was out of control and we were sitting in that dark bar drinking those rum-and-Cokes.

I wanted to tell John David, looky here, we're in Missouri having bar drinks and no one asked us about our damn IDs, let's just go to the burlesque, but the best I could do was give him a hard look and hope he got the message, but from the way he was squirming next to the nigger girl I didn't think he was getting any message other than the one she was delivering underneath the table. I could see her left arm moving back and forth sometimes like the piston on an old steam engine.

I was still thinking we could catch the burlesque, which I knew had shows up until midnight, but then the nigger girl said she wanted to ride with us back to Osawatomie and I could not for the life of me figure out what for. When John David didn't squash that idea outright, I knew we had a problem. That whole damn night was going screwy only I didn't have half an idea just how screwy it could get.

1954

We were visiting the Carlsons. The grownups played pinochle and we all had popcorn and Coca-Cola in skinny, sweating spun-aluminum drinking tumblers, green and orange and blue. The Carlsons had two kids, Nancy and Bubby. Nancy was between me and Larry, pretty, and I think Larry liked her.

The four of us kids were out on the back porch, sipping on Cokes, telling ghost stories, when we heard sirens. We looked off toward where they seemed to be heading and that's when we saw an orange glow in the sky, over some houses and trees. The breeze carried a smell too.

We called the grownups to the back door where they too could see the flickering orange light in the southeastern night sky and feel the smoke in their noses.

We all crowded into the Carlsons' car, a large new Buick, and Mr. Carlson drove to within a block or two of the fire, where we joined the knots of onlookers spilled out in a large curve around a small wooden house engulfed in flames.

We were in a colored neighborhood, down near the rail yard. It was a poor section of town with small wooden houses in need of fresh paint, without shingles or siding, and droopy porches that gave onto dirt front yards with hardly any grass and broken toys scattered around.

Firemen stood around in clusters aiming powerful jets of water at the burning house. The water appeared to evaporate before it reached the solid wall of fire.

Above the surprisingly loud noise of the fire rang a wail that was not from a siren or any other machine. A colored woman, held by several other women, strained toward the fire. The wail came from her open mouth. Although I saw her there and heard the noise I still struggled to believe that the noise I heard came from that person, that it was even a human noise at all.

Word passed through the crowd that a child was still inside the house, which by now looked like it was encased in a piece of violently shimmering orange-red cellophane.

When the talk reached our group, my Mama said something to my Daddy and he said something to Mr. Carlson, who looked at his wife, us kids, and the next thing, we're all headed back to the Buick. People were still streaming toward the fire, hurrying past us, their eyes reflecting the red and orange and yellow flames like small twinkling Christmas lights.

The next day at school Jaimie leaned over and whispered, the burned baby was Sharon Marie's cousin.

Across the classroom Sharon Marie sat stiffly at her desk in the row along the windows. She stared at something up front. Bright sunlight angled across her and a perfect silver line outlined her in profile.

I hadn't seen her when we all stood on the street corner and watched the house burn, but I hadn't been looking for her.

John David, said Mrs. Friedman, are you having trouble paying attention to what I'm saying? Is there something you think the class should see?

I remember saying, Sharon Marie's baby cousin got burned up last night and I saw it.

As soon as my words had hit atmosphere they'd turned sour even to my ears. My heart sunk and I felt like yelling, I'm sorry I'm sorry I'm sorry, but of course I did not. I don't know why I said it. At the moment I said it I felt, for just the briefest of seconds, like I had some special knowledge about Sharon Marie and if I let it go I would be announcing something like some kind of connection.

Mrs. Friedman jerked, and her expression instantly went from shock through brief anger at me for saying it through concern for Sharon Marie and then to pain when she met Sharon Marie's eyes.

Hissed Martha, dummy

It's the truth, I whispered back.

Oh, I'm so sorry, Sharon Marie, said Mrs. Friedman. Are you okay? Do you want to go home?

My little brother burned up too last night, Mrs. Friedman, said the Catholic kid. Can I go home?

Be quiet, she snapped. I want no more of that, do you hear?

It was quiet. Mrs. Friedman looked down at her desktop, her hands joined, elbows on the desk, like she was getting ready to pray. She glanced up at the Catholic kid, then over toward Sharon Marie, who was still staring straight ahead.

Come here, Mrs. Friedman said to Sharon Marie, motioning with her hand. Sharon Marie just looked at the hand waving at her from across the classroom, but then after a few moments rose a little awkwardly and walked toward Mrs. Friedman, who rose and took her hand and led her into the cloakroom. We could hear whispering and some crying, more soft talk, then silence.

We were quiet as mice, straining to hear whatever could be heard, then, as time passed and it seemed nothing more was to be heard, restless movement grew to whispering, which grew louder, into words you could hear, and then more noise, and then someone giggled, which briefly quieted the room before the noise returned when Mrs. Freeman didn't pop back into the room.

And then she was there, standing just inside the room, her arms folded, and her mouth set into a tight line, her eyes burning us with their glare.

We didn't know what to do so we did nothing, sitting as still as I can remember us ever sitting. It was like we knew that anything could set off something no one wanted to face.

I kept asking myself why seeing Sharon Marie so upset upset me so much, why I was stealing looks at her, why I was thinking about her at all. What was I supposed to do anyway?

I looked hard at my desktop, noticed where someone had scratched a few lines into the surface. I thought it could be the initials JB but I wasn't sure. I ran my finger over the scratches and thought hard about nothing in particular.

Sharon Marie didn't return that day or the next, but she came back right after that and never said anything about it, even when I asked her. She said it was done and she didn't see no reason to talk on it, her eyes pooled with damp stars. Something inside me fell apart and I knew I'd messed up bad when I'd blurted out what I had in class that day. It hadn't been no secret but I'd been the one to say it aloud and to have all our eyes turned to her grief. In her eyes I'd become one of the other kids, separated from her, even using her pain to advance my worth as someone who knew things no one else did.

I felt ashamed and I had no idea how to undo what was done. I did not know how to earn back the trust I'd too easily thrown away.

SUMMER/1855

O ur second summer was the summer the gypsies came to town. We heard them long before we saw them. Simon was helping me gather some potatoes and turnips for the stew Mama planned to make and we were down in what would become the far field, near the road, although calling those twin ruts a road was an elevation, if you ask me.

Something nagged at me and when I looked up I could see Simon looking all around, puzzlement on his face, his eyes roaming.

You hear that, he asked.

I nodded my head, though I didn't know quite what I was hearing, but I guessed it was the same thing that caught his attention.

What is it?

Don't know, I said.

We were both of us looking around though I was pretty sure it was coming from over the slight rise east of us.

Sounds like something breaking, glass or something, but it just keeps going, keeps on breaking, you know what I mean?

I nodded my head and started walking slowly toward the rise, where the sound was now clearly coming from. It did sound like glass, a tinkling but steady and constant, not stopping the way something that falls and breaks stops, the sound sudden like and then dribbling to nothing, all in a flash. Well, this sound just kept going, and it was getting louder as whatever it was got closer.

Then the head of a horse or maybe a mule came into sight from over the rise and then there was a covered wagon, and two people sitting on the box. It wasn't a regular covered wagon. The canvas stretched over the hoops was painted and there were poles sticking out with scarves and shiny things dancing on the ends and I could see it was the shiny things that were making the noise as the wagon rolled and jostled along the uneven ruts.

What do you make of that, asked Simon. He'd come up and joined me.

We were standing close together, watching the wagon as it neared where we stood.

The bright scarves blew in the wind. The noise sometimes mixed together in some way and music drifted to us but then the wind tossed it away.

Simon bumped me, like he wanted more room, but I didn't feel like moving and so we jostled and bumped and then leaned into each other, like we were having a kind of tug-o-war. Heat roiled off him, all along my side. As usual, he was annoying me but I didn't feel like allowing him his way so I stood firm, we'd just look silly, two people trying to occupy the same place.

They were gypsies, I was sure of it. Back in Tennessee we'd heard stories about gypsies. If the word gypsy come up then Mama or one of the older boys would talk about things they'd heard or knew of, how they were worse than niggers and even Jews. They'd steal anything that wasn't nailed down. Mama whispered to me once she'd heard that some went into a town back home and when they left two babies were gone, just disappeared and when the townsfolk caught up with the gypsies there weren't no babies there, those babies had been used in some devil's potions and were gone now for good. The gypsies were strung up, all of them, even the young'uns because they'd just grow up and turn into what they were and no one wanted to set loose baby killers so they were all hung dead.

But I was not afraid. Their wagon looked worse than ours, its wheels wobbled so severely I expected them to fall off right at my feet. They were close enough now to see their faces, dark eyes and dark hair and dark skin, but not nigger dark, just dark like an Indian but with more gray mixed in.

They looked like poor folks who'd stumbled onto a box of discarded party costumes, their faces were lined and had seen hard times, you could tell, but their shirts had bright patterns and they wore vests and necklaces and bracelets and jewels dangled from their ears, the man too.

Simon took a step away and my whole side was damp and chilled in the sudden air.

I saw the man say something and soon the curtain parted and three younger faces poked out from the wagon, a boy, two girls, about our age, and we five appraised each other as the wagon tinkered by, the man nodding greetings, the woman smiling and nodding as well, but the other three only watched us stare at them in wide-eyed wonder, these dark visitors, the girls the two most beautiful girls I'd ever in my life seen and the boy a foreign prince I was right then ready to pledge my life to like a brown god. There was something in his eyes that nearly lifted me off my feet. And we all looked at each other, that is to say, I did not only match stares with the gypsy prince, but looked at his sisters and Simon the prince, and at once I knew that somehow we were all looking at ourselves and each other, that I was seeing myself as he saw me, as the girls saw me, as Simon saw me, as I saw Simon and the girls, the boy, for the instant it takes to burst a soap bubble was how long we shared our thoughts as though one thought, one shared moment of the world, of ourselves, and more secrets were let out than anyone could monitor, and I knew the boy's wants and his fears and his ambitions, and the girls, their anger and their desires, and Simon's confusion and misery.

The wagon passed us, the man intent on the road ahead, the woman returning her attention ahead, her smile flattened out, we broke looks, the boy and the girls gone from view, but then as the wagon went away, the back curtain parted and there they were, the three, and we watched each other get smaller and smaller and still no one of us raised a hand or called out or even smiled.

The noise faded and the dust settled back and the light returned to normal.

I promised myself that if I had another chance, I would talk to the gypsies. They didn't seem evil to me, just poor and dirty and lost and truly no different from us except for the clothes.

Whenever I thought about them later, in my mind they floated, untethered, almost as free as birds.

We were torn whether to say anything to Mama or Papa about the gypsies. Simon said Papa'd be angry just knowing they were about, that we'd stood there like lumps and watched them.

We shoulda done something, he said.

And what would that have been, our brother? You wanted the two of us to leap on them and haul them to town and see to it they get strung up? Is that what you think we shoulda done?

Simon looked at me like I was a dumb puppy, or maybe just a dumb girl, his face impatient and darkened; if I'd a been the puppy, he'd have kicked me. I came to know that his life demanded action— even if it meant running in circles—while mine sought understanding.

You want them to run off with Baby Jonah?

I could not tell if he was angry or frightened or just annoyed I wasn't seeing the obvious, that we had been all that had stood between them gypsies and our baby brother getting snatched off the porch. His eyes were wide and filled with something, the anger or tears or some other thing you could tell he didn't quite have a handle on.

Did they look dangerous to you, Simon? Did they look like they wanted to snatch us up? I didn't feel like putting up with his guff this day; the gypsies had seemed about as dangerous to me as our milk cow.

You don't know nothing, he said, turning away and heading back toward the house with his armload of turnips and potatoes.

Your answer to everything is that no one but you knows a thing which is about as stupid as you could be, our brother; there's things you have no understanding of and one of these days you're gonna insist on the wrong thing to the wrong folks and they gonna straighten you out like a wet stick.

He hadn't stopped or looked back or done anything that gave away he heard me at all but I knew he had because his every muscle seemed taut and he walked with that angry stiffness both he and Papa retreated to when their humor was our of sorts.

I stayed back, tried to calm my mind, and soon found myself staring up the road, toward where the gypsies had come from, like I expected more to appear. I was pretty sure I'd hear them before I first saw the top of their wagon or maybe some colored flag mounted on a long pole.

After a bit I realized I'd pivoted and I was staring after the ones that had passed, could no longer hear them and they'd disappeared in some dip in the land or maybe they'd just ascended to some star. They'd looked like angels; I admit, scruffy angels, angels down on their luck, perhaps homeless or lost or dirt poor angels trying to find their way back home.

I gathered my things, a half bushel of potatoes bunched in my apron, and shuffled back up the slope. It seemed much darker than it had been just a minute ago. I wondered how long I had stood at the road.

All the faces available turned toward me when I walked in the door. Only Baby Jonah's sweet pink face was absent, him sleeping in his crib. From their faces I felt like I'd brought home an armload of rats.

When I found Simon he bounced his eyes to Papa who looked tired and sad and troubled.

I have heard that gypsies were on the road, he said. Is that true, Sarah?

Yes, Papa.

He was quiet, carefully picking out his words, guiding them through his tempers, making sure his mind was doing the choosing and not his heart.

Why didn't you come get me, daughter?

I caught a flickering motion to the side, Mama's head moving from me to Papa and back. I did not dare make notice. I continued to look straight at Papa.

I could not take my eyes off them, Papa. Their wagon was strung with glass and colored scarves and I did not want to miss any of it.

Simon was with me, I said. I weren't alone. Neither was he.

I could see him thinking about that, that of all our choices—me leaving Simon alone by the road, or Simon leaving me, or us both leaving—nothing was clear, no best answer jumped up.

You know about gypsies, he said. We don't want them around. They can't be trusted. They are dangerous.

I didn't think they looked even a bit dangerous but I kept that to myself. They looked poor and hungry and generally worse off than us. Maybe that made them dangerous, they'd want what they didn't have, what they saw around them out in the middle of nowhere. It was hard to say, looking around this country, that people had much to do with how things were—it all mostly looked like it always had with maybe some fields scraped into the ground here and there, some buildings, some ruts deemed roads, a small collection of tents and one-room cabins together making up a town, but everywhere around, everywhere else was tall grasses and crooked cottonwoods and black jack oaks and blackberry thickets and rocks of every size. Not untamed or wild so much as unaltered, unaffected like we'd all just showed up and made a few scratches but from way up on some imaginary hill those scratches could not be seen, might as well not be there. And coming into that kind of rawness, gypsies—or settlers from Tennessee or whoever—could look around and say to themselves with some conviction, This might as well be mine.

Word was, Simon said, the gypsies were in town and had things to sell. Neighbor men—Mr. Wilkinson from east down Mosquito Creek, Mr. Doumas from the next place south, Mr. Pomeroy, next place after that—had been coming around on their horses—no hurry-up gallops, no horse and rider coming to a noisy dirt-kicking stop or the like, but men rode up the road and turned into our farm and sought out Papa and they'd talk, their heads leaned toward each other, as though to catch every word, make no mistakes about it. Drury and William joined them and they too leaned in, like tented rifles.

If I wandered too close the neighbor man—whoever it was— would look at me and shut up and then give Papa a look, a scowl, and Papa'd remind me of some job I had to do, some place I had to go, and I'd go and as soon as I was far enough away their heads edged closer and they started in again.

That night after dinner, Papa said we were going to town in the morning, there were things we needed and things that needed done.

Simon's eyes went wide, his back stiffened.

William and Drury will be with me, Mahala; you'll have Simon and Sarah for the little one or if you need things carried.

His look was the one he gets when he had to tell us bad news, some favorite lamb or chicken had been killed. Or we were leaving Tennessee.

I could tell that Mama wanted to say something. The words were so far along you could see them fighting to get out of her mouth, her whole face twisting to keep still.

Papa, I started, is this about the gypsies?

He didn't say a thing, but looked at me like I'd broken something and then his eyes raised to the ceiling and he let out a big breath no one knew he'd been holding in, and the room filled with something new, a kind of light that didn't call attention to itself but made everything glow just enough to make it all seem a cloud had moved away overhead except that this was night and our only light was the two lamps and three or four candles Mama and I put around. But the extra light was truly no more than a log flared up or some such thing.

There are things in this world, Sarah, that simply do not concern you. You are blessed enough to have three older brothers and your Papa to keep you safe. Your concerns are here, with your Mama and your baby brother.

But, yes, our daughter, it is about the gypsies.

He was peering into me and inside I was crying out why, why these people, they look like you and Mama and Simon, like us they were white or certainly white enough given the range of white folk I had seen in my short life, white men from places I could only dream on but they each talked different, each had a different look on things but they each knew without a doubt that they were white. In my life it has been the niggers and the Indians and everyone else, and we were in the everyone else group, all us kinds of white people from all around the world, and now Papa was telling me that there were white people that were better or worse than other white people, and I just didn't know how I could know, it seemed I would have to concentrate on and keep track of kinds of shades or features or gestures or clothes or shoes or hats, wagons. Why did we bother? What had they done or what would they do?

What is wrong with them? I blurted. Simon stared at me, his mouth open, but no one else took their eyes of Papa, waiting on his words.

They are dishonest people, daughter. Thieves and liars and cheats. They know no moral bounds.

Simon suddenly burst out, gypsies steal babies and cut out they hearts and drink their blood!

Papa dropped his eyes to the table briefly but then raised up his head and said to Simon, boy, I do not know where you hear your stories, I do not know who fills your head with the nonsense you entertain, but I want you to stop sharing it with the rest of us. I cannot keep you from thinking what you think but I can keep you from letting us in on it. You will either stop spending time with those troublemakers I know you talk to, or you keep their nonsense to yourself, and then there will be no more wild talk, do you understand me, Simon?

Simon nodded, said, yes, Papa.

Mama, didn't you tell me you thought gypsies were some kind of Christian, I said.

Sarah, Papa said, his voice sharp and hard. I felt his eyes burning me. Your mother does not have to explain anything to you; it is enough I said what I said, and you will scrub out these fancied ideas about gypsies or any other of that type. They are not like us and no one here wants them around. Not just us Southerners either but the free-staters too.

They looked as dangerous as kittens, Papa.

Papa looked at me, a kind of sadness creeping into his eyes from the corners.

Maybe you don't recall your hands scratched and bleeding from playing with kittens, Sarah, he said. I do.

After supper Simon was sent to fetch fresh water. I stepped out to shake blankets and joined him as he walked to the well with the bucket.

What do you think is going to happen, I asked.

He looked straight ahead into the dark, his eyes roaming as though something might step out of the night blackness.

I don't know, he finally said. Something.

You telling me Drury or William didn't say nothing to you about this? I know you boys better than that, Simon.

We were at the well and Simon lowered the fill bucket into the hole, glancing at me.

There's talk, he said.

I know there's talk, our brother. Any darned fool knows that. What I want to know is what the talk is about. We both know what happened to the gypsies back home, what they'd done to them—

—They's baby killers, Sarah, he said, turning to me full. They sacrificed babies to the devil.

And you know this how? I heard no babies were found, alive or dead. How do you know gypsies had anything to do with them missing babies?

Babies do not disappear, Sarah. His tone said he was talking to a child that needed help understanding even the simple things.

In a way I knew he was right. Not about the gypsies, but babies didn't just disappear. It seemed to me there was too much I didn't know. Was there some band of cutthroats passing through at the same time but because the gypsies were there they received all the attention? Maybe wolves got them babies, or they wandered off and fell down some hole, someone's untended well. I just did not know, I decided.

And neither did Simon.

But everyone seemed ready to blame the gypsies for everything that went wrong in their lives and that didn't make sense to me. I know when I learn something has been done wrong my first thought is that Simon had something to do with it and if it ain't him then it's Drury or even William, them boys have enough mischief stored up between them to cause trouble the rest of someone's life, they're like pups who think that all life is romping and ripping things up. But I am also wrong often enough to show me that not all my judgments fall on the right side of right.

Going into town was always exciting, and I relished it in ways I did not understand, but something about the added people and animals stirred up the noise so there was an all-the-time rumble and hum that scored the bustle tween stores and wagons and horses and mules, and its tune led me around like the piper as I marveled over time at the town growing up from nothing, like watching a calf grow into a young bull.

It affected us all and each trip into town started earlier and brighter than our regular days, the boys spreading out like spilled water, their morning tasks divided up and hurried through, Mama and me getting the fire going, a pot of porridge under way and bread warming.

We sat around the table eating, no lost time talking, then our clothes tidied up, our hair slicked or brushed, the wagon loaded with the things we wanted to sell at market, Mama carefully repeating to herself the list of stores we needed, flour, molasses, dried beans, tobacco, coffee, thread, hemp rope, a blanket, if there was one nice enough for how much Mama had tucked away, and then with Drury and William on horses and the rest of us in the wagon with Papa holding the reins, we headed off to Osawatomie.

We were about an hour or so away and it never went fast enough even though I deeply loved the ride, the steady warm jounce as Mama and Simon and I jiggled and rubbed under the blankets we'd thrown over us to keep off the morning chill—the sun wouldn't be any higher than a finger or two and the night air still had bite to it so we huddled together separated by our different blankets and we giggled and laughed the first minutes until the humor wore off and then I'd settle into the ride's rhythm and watch the east sky flare up, red streaks the width of the morning horizon and then them turning to a city girl's pink and all around the rest of the sky going from deep blue to some kind of watery green when the sun is almost ready to show before settling into the day's robin's egg blue.

My friends, outside of Simon, were often in town with their families on Saturdays and we'd walk around on the edges of things and talk without Mama or Papa or some brother listening. It was a treat, a sweet letting go of myself those brief meetings but not all were so effective as sometimes, for some law written by some evil part of God, boys would pester us, tease us, talk about us loudly, kick pebbles at our boots, come in real close and say something sassy and then dart away, and I never knew what it was I was supposed to do, how I was supposed to act. I wanted to hit them, I wanted to laugh with them, I wanted the freedom they had to dance around and say things too loud, the right they had to do what they wanted.

I was lost inside myself, considering how to handle the boys, when I got my first peek of town, smoke gathering a few rises away. If the wind was up, the smoke'd make a dark smudge that lightened as it rolled away from town, but not today. It hung over the town like a threadbare blanket. Off the side, broken, abandoned wagon parts—shattered wheels or yokes—discarded oddities, pieces of furniture, scraps of cloth and the like, and the road itself a little wider, ruts settling into a kind of levelness, the land cleared here and there, then a cabin and then a collection of tents and more cabins, a real house, larger buildings going up, in various stages, one, maybe two, looking like more than one story, horses and wagons tied up on both sides of the street, people shuffling along, calling greetings, talking, tipping hats, shaking hands, bowing heads, smiling, and always movement everywhere you looked, wagons unloaded, loaded, riders coming, children often getting in the way.

And it was then I noticed there weren't any children chasing after something, no shouting or laughing, whistles, no dust raised that wasn't raised by a horse. Then I saw two, the Frederick kids, Harry and Sebastian, seated quietly in a wagon, heads down, their backs bowed, broad brimmed hats covering their faces, hunched inward, their mama sitting there too her head stiff and even and her eyes locked on something so hard to see it made her eyes red and her face hard.

I saw others, a string of Smiths, all them brothers and sisters holding hands and the lead one, the eldest, Louise, a daughter just shy my age, pulled steadily along in her mama's grip, but when she saw me she eased her struggling and looked down and wouldn't look at me.

Things smelled different. There were always the cook smells in town, bacon and bread and coffee, and the animals and, well, just everything else that can be imagined. Overall it smelled exciting and cheery, but today beneath that was something sour that made you want to turn your eyes away even though it wasn't something to see. It was like a fog that could not be seen but was there and that enfolded the town and it mixed itself with the town and there rose an odor from the living things, the smell of something like stomach bile or rotting cabbage or something grown black deep inside, and as I looked around it seemed that everyone's faces were pinched tight, from the smell or from seeing something or hearing something they didn't want to know about but was pushed into their faces anyway.

I knew every bit of it was about the gypsies, it was so clear there should have been a banner across the main street saying, The Gypsies Are Here, or What's To Be Done About the Gypsies.

My strongest desire at that moment was to go home, to be almost anywhere but there. Fear and hate were so mixed with the air it was one and we all breathed it in and it got inside us and we shared it but instead of drawing strength and bravery from our shared thing we became more fearful, more hateful because we saw what we were or what we could become and it felt like something big was sitting on me, crushing me. My head felt pushed in. I was sure that if the wagon stopped and I got down, I'd sink into some kind of molasses. If Mama asked me to hold something for her, I'd drop it, my hands felt swollen, useless mitts. My eyes puffed closed. My body bloated, filled up with sick air and I floated off like a circus balloon.

But of course I did not, I sat on the wagon bench and watched men talk in close groups, gesturing like they were in rooms and not out in the street where even the little children could see.

I knew then that what I saw that day would stay with me for as long as I lived. And I also knew that I would spend years and years trying everything I could to make the memory go away.

Papa nodded politely to other menfolk and Mama smiled at the women. Papa halted the wagon halfway between the general store and the blacksmith's at the south end of town. Mama and Simon and me took Baby Jonah and made our way to the general store, and Papa and the boys walked back the way we came to join a circle of men gathered near the land office though it weren't but half built, white granite stones the size of dogs, sent all the way from New York State by one of them abolitionists with too much money and not enough back there to keep him busy.

The general store had only been up for a month, maybe less, and was the biggest building in town, two large real glass windows on each side of double doors, wide so you could get out the big floppy gunnysacks, feed or flour, sugar, some of the tools Mr. Jenkins kept.

Both doors were open and the inside was crowded with women and their little ones, some girls I knew, all bunched in there, the voices blended together and made a noise like a mountain on a summer night, all the things trying to out-do the other.

I saw two friends over in one corner, both still with mouths turned down before they saw it was me, then Mary Sue lifting her hand and tendering a itty-bitty wave, her hand dropping back to join the other, her eyes noting it like it was important. I waved back but then Mama tugged on my sleeve and Simon and I helped her gather our supplies on the long counter that ran the whole side of the store, next to the other piles of things, the other women talking softly to each other, Mr. Jenkins and his wife bustling here and there, locating things or totaling up or taking orders, working out trades, settling accounts.

The gypsies were weighing heavily upon everything around us, you could feel it in the store, all the talk you heard, though I saw Mr. Jenkins frown and shake his head, his eyes undecided about whether to flash anger or cry. But all his headshaking and even the every-now-and-then humph didn't slow the worried talk, some frightened about what the gypsies'd do, some frightened about what's gonna get done to the gypsies, and there were some words about that difference too, some hard looks, some times when the talk did in fact stop as one set of women glared at another, some interior resolution made or violated. It felt like it did back home in the moments before William or Drury'd lop the head off our supper that day, before the headless chicken ran itself dry, my brothers scattering and whooping like wild Indians.

Mr. Jenkins pointed out someone had business to conduct and that it was him and his wife and if people didn't have business, to take themselves outside so's they didn't get in the way of those that had come here for a purpose other than gossip, thank you.

We were in there a while but then we were done and after Simon and I got all our purchases moved to the wagon and tucked away under a blanket, we were free to explore until time to leave, hours away.

My friends were standing together outside the store, holding hands and not looking noticeably happier.

Hello Mary Sue, hello Virginia, I said. I tried to make my smile bigger than it felt but that never works without it showing you working at it too hard.

They gave me the same smile back, but that made me smile bigger, this time reaching my eyes and I was truly pleased to see them. They each said my name and we were okay again.

What is going on, asked Mary Sue. She was the youngest of us but by only a half year or about. You know there's gypsies camped just on the other side of town.

Virginia nodded her head in agreement.

I saw them yesterday, I said. Inside I was disappointed how good it had felt to say that as though I had something to do with them being here.

You seen the gypsies? Virginia said, making it sound like I done something wrong and she admiring it at same time.

I hear something terrible is gonna happen to them gypsies, she said, her mouth set grave but her eyes twinkling.

All my warm feelings for Mary Sue and Virginia were cooling. It surprised me how roiled I was inside, how what folks were saying was stirring me up. I didn't understand. I was scared. I didn't know who I was right then.

And what was it the gypsies did to you or yours? I nailed her with my eyes.

You'd have thought I'd slapped her, the way her head jolted, her eyes sprang open, her mouth made a little O, her right hand even moving partway toward her face, to rub a bruise that wasn't there.

Sarah Dawson, why are you being mean to Mary Sue, asked Virginia. You're not an ignorant fool. Your mama and papa done told you about gypsies and niggers and Jews and all the other things you got to watch out for in this world. It is not a sweet place, Sarah Dawson, your wishing aside. Them gypsies have got to go on. They are not wanted here. Only bad things will happen.

Oh, I have no doubt about that, I said. I suppose the question is, will it be the gypsies or the townsmen who do the bad things first.

I was still deciding whether I did in fact want to smack both their faces, knock their daddies' words out, see what it was their true heart felt. Did they, could they, truly hate these people who had done nothing, who had just showed up like themselves had once showed up, stuffed into a wagon, their whole world in trunks and boxes, everything wrapped up in blankets and rope, creaking and tossing along down some awful rutted road, you thinking the wheels could pop off any moment and every now and then one does and you're lucky you aren't killed cause some are. Or there's other things too, highway robbers or Indians or runaway slaves or gangs of boys inflamed from someone's daddy's corn licker, looking for some poor folk to mistreat.

Don't they remember being scared and surrounded by loneness? I knew with certainty that it had shifted things inside me. The world no longer unfolded in a regular way, I noticed the newness of more things, the differences that prove uniqueness is everything and then knowing that it is men who catalog and grade and count and arrange and kill with names.

If we take away the names we'd have to see the thing itself and then there could be no denying differences. We are just an equal part of the whole thing, all rocks in the wall, all grains of sand.

The trip from Tennessee showed me more than just all them trees and hills and rivers and small towns and such. I saw how we were, out there twixt the place we'd been and the place we were gonna be, nowhere, really, our world was what we could see around us, but getting closer to one side, further away from the other, pushing what we could see further west, pulling in the dark behind us, the things behind us of no matter, better forgotten, if we could. What was ahead of us was what mattered, what we had to focus on.

What we met on the road seemed like a preview of our future though I knew it was different, knew the folks we passed heading the other way, toward where we'd been, were leaving for a reason, like we were, and I wondered what it was, what took them away from the territories, away from the future. I understood that my future wasn't the same as Mary Sue's or Papa's or Simon's or anyone's except when there's some overlap. I knew I hadn't walked in those folks' shoes, I knew I knew nothing about their lives but I could not help believe we were the ones going forward and they the ones going back, not to.

I marveled that though we were each pointed in different directions and toward different lives, different everything, at that moment when we passed on the road, edging one wagon by the other—no one could afford to bump the other—and we nodded at each other, sometimes said a greeting, asked about the weather up the road, at that moment when we were side-by-side, we were equal parts of the same picture, impossible to tell from inside the picture who was going where, and then we were by and I knew that if any them would turn and watch us rattle away, they'd see what I saw looking back if I looked, the covered-hoop shape of the back of the wagon, the dark hole in the middle, and the face of the girl looking at the face of the girl in the other covered-hoop wagon opening.

Didn't Mary Sue or Virginia ever look back on their way here? Didn't they think on such things?

Where did you girls get these notions?

They looked at each other and then both at me, their eyes and mouths fixed into lines, their flesh gone hard, they could have been looking in some surprise at something one of them would have to step on or crush with a rock. I was no longer Sarah but had become their bothersome little brother or a dog that wouldn't stay away.

You are the one with the peculiar notions, Sarah Dawson, said Mary Sue. Virginia was back to nodding her head, Mary Sue's words good enough for her.

You don't think you're better than them gypsies? I know I am.

Mama said they were Christian, just like me and you, I said.

Well, I don't know, said Mary Sue. She didn't like hearing that and I could see her stumbling on herself working on the thing to say about that.

Maybe they ain't truly Christians, said Virginia. Maybe they are just acting like they are Christians to fool us, so's they can get close to us, so's we won't suspect them being what they in fact are.

Oh, you could see how pleased she was developing that theorem, how she swelled with pride.

Oh, phooey, look around you, there are a whole lot of folk pretending to be Christian, way I look at it, I said. They read the Bible and they go to meetings and they say all the things you are supposed to say if you are Christian, but you watch the way they live, the way they take care of themselves and the ones they're with, they love, and after a while, you watch enough, you see they aren't so Christian, they are just saying the words and agreeing each other are all Christian but their true lives are mean and angry and filled with the kind of thing no real Christian would countenance.

You must be talking about your family, Sarah Dawson, because you sure ain't talking about mine, said Mary Sue, then noting the look on Virginia's face, look that said she wanted to be included on the good side of things. Or Virginia's, she added.

There was no doubt in my mind or in my heart that I was right but I still felt unnecessarily cruel. Mary Sue and Virginia were friends and I did not have all that many. I knew their stance on niggers—they were brought here by their papas and mamas from Southern states, Mary Sue from Tennessee like us and Virginia from her namesake, and when she'd told me her name first time, and that she was named after the state, I'd said, It's a good thing your mama didn't have you in Kentucky, then, and she'd just looked at me, puzzled but certain I'd said something ill of her.

We don't have to argue about this, I said. Let's just take a look, you say they're south of town. Let's stroll down that way, maybe skirt around them two new buildings, see what they look like in back, wander on from there. There's three of us and all the men are right here, a holler away. We'll be safe.

I heard they can put women in spells, Virginia nearly whispered.

Spells? What kind of spells?

Trances, like you was dead or under some kind of devil's power.

Virginia, I said, I truly don't think there is anything you can be made to do if you do not want to do it, least not through spells or potions or curses or any other kind of nonsense. Nobody is gonna stare into your eyes and capture your spirit with a wink or a set of fancy words, not unless that's what you want too, unless you're saying you're a fool can be talked into anything. Is that it, are you frightened we'll get down there and of one of them gypsies will whisper some magic words and you will go all limp and be carried away to wherever gypsies hide their little girl prisoners. Those'd be some special words, I grant that. I'd like to know a few words like that. In fact, for words such as that I'd just about be bold enough to ask about them words, be worth the chance if in the end I got them words to use for my own. I could come back here, Virginia, and when you were standing in front of the general store, thinking about your buying list, I'd slip next to you and whisper them words into your ear and in a blink you'd be under my control. I could make you do anything, I could make you go with me and Mary Sue to see the gypsies, couldn't I. I could get us all down there, see for ourselves what they are about. I want to know for myself and I want you to see for yourselves too, Virginia and Mary Sue.

Come on, let's go, I said.

They stared at me, a little open eyed, and then we all kind of snickered, a nervous snicker to be sure, but it was the closest to laughter we would get right then and it was enough. I chanced a smile, not at all certain they weren't angry.

They ducked their heads but everything I'd seen before their faces were hidden said smile so I reckoned we were fine or fine enough to continue.

We started.

1960

Dorthea

I was thirsty and had a bunch a troubles and I didn't have no money and that's when I seen these two white boys standing around, they heads together like they's hatching some deep plot, something dangerous, which I knew they wasn't, just looking at them, all clean and white and lost from somewhere, you could just see it, like a label hanging up in the air.

At the least, I could get a drink or two. Better'n that, I thought I could get something extra, for Delbert, figured I could dream up something, get a few bucks, without even having to take them to no hotel or nothing.

And if I had to do that, well, I do it and count the money in the morning, my lucky night downtown, bail Delbert's ass out next day.

The tall one, John David—one of them boys got to use two names, like one can't say it all—he was nice, looked me in the eye, paid attention to what I said. The other one, Woody—is that a real name?—I caught him making eyes at my tits about every chance he got, mumbling to himself, and I thought was one a them doesn't like negroes, he just ain't said it out loud, so far.

Delbert was heavy on my mind, got hisself in the lockup again, sitting in the city jail for smart-mouthing a cop, some white man's idea of a crime. He innocent, like he always was. That boy makes me laugh and cry at the same time. Mama ruined that boy. But he family and I reckoned it was my duty to get him out of there.

I could sure used some help that night. But those boys didn't worry me none.

I was just gonna take them for a little ride.

1855

Overhead a black dot swooped, grew large enough to become a crow, then a smart cut and there it was, flattened out into a long, long glide across the tents and roughed out buildings and townspeople. It flew side to side, turning one eye to the ground then the other, carving up what was to be seen, what was worth paying attention to, what was curious, what ticked some part of the bird's insides, made it angle off, start a slow wide circle, south of everything else, where startling colors drew the bird's eye, gave a marvelous swirl of sunrise and sunset flapping midair, appearing, disappearing, like rips in the air, colors leaking out, the crow circling and watching, circling, watching.

If I'd been that crow, I'd have seen us three girls slowly making our way south behind the stores, wagons, people, going slow so as to not draw attention but still scooting behind walls and barrels and wagons and piles of boxes, staying largely out of sight, snaking south, drawn now by something new in the mix that day, some soaring sweet song not made by any bird I knew of, we flew around one corner and then stopped dead as before us suddenly was the gypsy wagon, the horse untethered and grazing off right, a tentlike thing partway attached to the wagon jutted out, patterned walls, pictures, and from each tent pole hung waving banners and streamers of all the colors I'd never seen, every color invented danced in the wind.

The song came from the papa and the boy playing fiddles but not like anything I knew. This was slow and sad and didn't seem suited to dance but something you'd listen to, open up your heart to, tell secrets to, the twin notes wrapped you up and carried you like cherubs, and then the older gypsy girl started singing and the bottom of everything gave way, an immediate look into her soul that made me want to weep.

I felt transported but to where I was speechless to say. I didn't even know if this kind of thing had a name, were there words available to tell about this, could I even think on it or was it something that owned me because it owned my feelings, taken me over and set everything vibrating.

I looked at Virginia and Mary Sue and saw they were equally as transfixed. The music united us, the three of us and the gypsies, I knew this. We reached as one and joined hands and then we glanced looks at each other and then back at the tent and the blowing colors and then we smiled when it was clear to us that the swirling scarves were in fact another instrument and it seemed as obvious as noting the black cloud before a rainstorm but we were still enough our regular old selves that we knew this was something out of the ordinary for us, that it was something closer to visions, to being touched by God, that we trembled in a quiet, exhilarated fear that a line had been crossed.

I wondered if our mamas and papas were right. These beautiful people and their beautiful music were exactly what true evil would look like, how it could get inside you and defeat your soul's best arguments. They would make music that grabbed you and made you imagine things.

But I was not having evil thoughts or even selfish thoughts or any thoughts that featured me at all. What was inside me the way air was inside me was the sound of the world God made and was as pure and innocent as any natural sound.

They had clothes that smelled like foreign countries and adornments that gleamed and reflected every piece of light that came near them, off their ears and wrists and fingers and waists and feet and here and there like tiny winking gods.

And they were just gypsies, my heart whispered, papa and mama and all the children, making a song like no one's heard, fiddles and a small odd-shaped guitar and the girls singing and banging their hands on little drums that tinkled from tiny bells.

Other folk had wandered toward the sound, some womenfolk in clumps and the men closest, keeping themselves between the gypsies and the women, the boys acting coltish, sucking on their lips, wiping their noses they were so excited and agitated, the men quieter but stern, some drunk.

At least no one has brought a rifle, I said.

There's enough of them I doubt they need more'n a few raised voices, said Mary Sue. What could they do?

They has powers, Virginia said quietly.

Oh, I can see that, I said, almost laughing. I heard it, anyway. It was everything you wanted music to be, holy and heartfelt and almost too pretty to bear. Whatever power it had it had because you willingly gave yourself to it; it would not, could not, take anything from you you didn't give away, and then it returned it to you, focused and arranged like a fancy restaurant table.

I did not want it to stop, and as two follows one and three two, I did not want these men to stop it.

I knew that if I looked at the men grouped at the end of town, facing the gypsy encampment and saw my papa I would be unable to do what I knew I had to do. Something.

I let loose my friends' hands and marched toward the gypsies, head and eyes ahead, mouth set firm, though the music did its best to thwart that with elevation. My hands were balled, my feet kicking up dust with my determined gait.

I let the music fill me up, used it to keep out all other sounds, my eyes sought and found the smallest thing I could see and it became my beacon, a shimmering silver necklace the boy wore around his neck, silver glinting the overhead sun, and tiny blues and greens and reds from other things set in the necklace, the closer I got the better I could see, saw the winking colors were from stones, saw the silver was etched and patterned, saw the pieces of the silver chain, and the sun reflecting off the heart of the piece of silver, and the swell of the fiddles and voices all filled me to where I knew I could, if I wanted, lift off and join the crow that circled overhead.

I was focused on the boy's necklace because I feared meeting his eyes but I must have looked because I can say that they were dark and shown like lanterns and that what I saw beyond that was a world opened up to me, a world where I belonged, where the things I felt listening to the music ordered all other things and there was balance and acceptance. There was rightness and it lifted me.

I realized I could not keep walking, unless it was my aim to cause a ruckus by walking until I tumbled into the boy and his fiddle and I knew that wouldn't do. I stopped, maybe ten feet from them, right in the middle of a ball of music and I could not stop myself when I noticed my head was bobbing like an apple in the wind, my head following the music, up and down, and I was riding the music.

It rose one last unbearable time, the boy and his papa flailing at their fiddles, their arms moving fast as whips, all the notes up and up and up, they sounded like bells, and then it stopped and the silence that was there for just a brief moment was crushed by the sound of my name.

Sarah.

It was my papa's voice.

The gypsy woman very slowly lowered her instrument and her eyes glowed and a knowing smile came to her mouth and she nodded to me, the nod pointing toward my papa.

I turned and he was right there, coming up fast like a spooked dog.

The silence was hard as stone, it stopped Papa like he'd walked into a solid wall.

I called your name, Sarah. Why didn't you stop?

Papa, I didn't hear you. The music was so loud, Papa, didn't you hear it? Wasn't it beautiful?

Piece by piece the silence broke apart, breathing and rustling, leather squeaking, snorting horses, hooves thumping, whispers, words, the fading hollow ring of one of the instruments, my own breathing, a slow tumbling of words wanting to get out, to explain but the thing that kept me silent was my awareness the music had not touched Papa at all.

I recognized my foolishness for thinking for a minute that there could be special circumstances under which the standard rules were suspended or worth revisiting. Whatever had happened to me had not happened to Papa and so it didn't matter, my reasons. I'd done something far more serious than listen to gypsy music.

He took my arm and steered me back toward the center of town. I saw Mary Sue's and Virginia's folks reeling them in as well, Mary Sue's ear firmly in the grip of her papa whose face was as red as a late radish.

I wanted to slap the faces that stared at me, but in a flash I was also ashamed, understanding that my actions allowed these men and women the freedom to embrace their hate. I would become their excuse to roust the gypsies. I'd shown how dangerous they were, how they could lure away children with the devil's song.

Or maybe they just felt weak and small against people who were so different, who didn't care about the things that mattered to them: standing your ground and putting roots into the soil and doing a full day's hard work and submitting to God; who seemed intentionally rootless passing through the land of the rooted. What leaves with the gypsy when the gypsy leaves, what goes with them, what have they taken? China? Hearts? Dreams? Boundaries?

From my world looking into theirs, gypsies seemed so restless, like there's some kind of tune whirling inside their heads all the time and not just when they pick up instruments, something that blurs the land so it looks the same standing still as it does rolling by on a wagon. No reason to pick one place over another, it all has the same hard, unwelcome color and design.

You have done it this time, daughter Sarah. We were moving about as fast together as I could've running full speed alone, my feet seemed to touch ground just every now and then, Papa striding big hunks, hauling me off like a runwild pony captured, the waste of time and embarrassment making him speed everything up, getting me out of there, the first mad steps in forgetting my behavior and still knowing that'll never happen. We could live here, the whole lot of us, for another hundred years and there will be folks who will see us, see me stooped and old and wrinkled and white and Papa long gone, just a memory and the first words that will appear in their minds will be, That is the girl who almost ran off with the gypsies, wasn't it her daddy the one almost let it happen?

The music had quieted them and then the silence and Papa's calling my name had been the only sound but as we moved through the townspeople, past neighbors and people whose faces we knew, after we'd gone by someone would whisper or say low, and the further we got away the louder they started to talk so by the time we were through them and Papa continued to pull me toward our wagon, voices raised, louder with each step, the odd thing us getting further and further away and it getting louder and louder so it was like we were in fact getting closer, the sound growing and them shrinking, and their interest shifting, turning their backs on us, looking back at the gypsies, dozens of black or near black, brown, dark colors, coats and dresses, a pale ribbon here and there but somehow looking like no more than thick shadows, and the gypsies, bathed in sunlight drawn to their gay colors making them look like celestials fending off the closing night.

Sarah, you are to turn your eyes away, right now, daughter. There is nothing for you to see. Papa's face loomed over me, a new shadow, the sun flaring around his head. I felt lifted away, the noisy voices behind me, a kind of crackling like limbs breaking away in a storm, the sunlight flowing around Papa's head, beams of light like arrows glancing all around me, surrounding Papa like a coat of fire, his shadow enveloping me, blocking the light, embracing me with its darkness, my eyes seeking Papa's, just my arm's length away. I felt his breath, its sourness suddenly sharp and clear, its sting rose into my eyes and tears started down my face, and then Papa quieted himself, leaned back, unblocked the sun and I was instantly washed in a brightness I was not ready for, had forgotten was there behind him and the world went white black, my eyes locking shut and behind my lids the world was red and black at once, there was no roaring, no light, no face, no sky, my eyes squeezed shut.

I heard crows, overhead, calling, calling, calling.

The next two Saturdays Papa made me stay home when the family went to town, Drury and Simon watching over me, giving them work on top of that, it all my fault their looks said, Simon sulking, refusing to even talk to me. No one those two weeks would talk about the gypsies to me at all.

In the dark at night I'd use my finger and trace in the air my mind's picture of the gypsy prince. I always saved his eyes for last, just before I drifted to sleep.

A heaviness sat over us or so it seemed to me but perhaps no one talking to me had something to do with that. I sunk into loneliness and knew I was up to my ears in self-pity but it was the warmest feeling I could generate so I held to it until I grew bored with it, about the time Papa said I could go with them the next day.

I felt like I'd been given a piece of hard candy.

Later, in bed, the night cold falling over us, I found myself in a turmoil that I had been so pleased to be asked to join the others in town. What had I done?

The ride into town was almost like all the others, maybe Simon was a little noisier, Papa and Mama and the older boys a little quieter, their own thoughts their own, and I said nothing, not even commenting on the sunrise which should have made me say something, it was what I did, describe to them what we all could see, but I knew they enjoyed my cleverness, so this time, when we all could see wide wavy bands of pinks and violets and faded greens, I believed I noticed heads tilted my way, a few eyes darting to mine, open mouths, arched brows, expressions that said, What did you say?

But I said nothing, did not have enthusiasm for it, decided they could see it plain as me, who needed words from me to sort it out?

I found myself thinking about the last time I'd been in the wagon, after the gypsies.

Mama sat with me, our backs to the south, our eyes staring at nothing, just half-done buildings and more wagons like ours, horses, the rutted street, shadows reaching east. After a bit, Papa returned with the other boys and without saying more than a word or two he turned the wagon and we headed back home.

You will keep your eyes pointed straight ahead, daughter, he said as we neared where we turned north out of town, the knot of townspeople still facing the gypsy camp.

We turned and pointed the horses toward home.

I could sense Simon twisting around, looking back, and I wanted with all my might to look, but I didn't dare, Papa had his face turned partway around, keeping his eye on me.

The ride home was quiet, not at all like usual, when we were normally burning with our separate stories from our day, each of us in a hurry to tell what we'd done or seen or talked about, but this time it was different, we'd seen the same common thing, like the sunrises, there was no secret about what we'd seen but it was covered with a silence that seemed as dark and thick as blankets.

My thoughts could not help but wander to a place where I knew that what I had seen, what I had done, was significantly different from what Papa and Mama and Simon and William and Drury had seen. I had felt something that they had not and though I did not then know what it was, I knew it was important and I knew that something deep in me had resettled in a new way. And I knew there'd be some getting used to it.

I strained my eyes right as far as I could without turning my head when we came to the place where there was a way to see the gypsies but I could not see very well, even at the edges, no banners or scarves, but the boys looked openly, then William and Drury snapped their eyes to Papa, Simon choosing me, puzzlement in his eyes.

They're gone, said Simon, almost whispering. Or moved.

Papa studied our path into town, you'd thought he hadn't heard a word.

We were quiet another few minutes and then Papa pulled the wagon over near the general store. It seemed to be a day without big greetings. The town had a kind of hush on it, like it had been told to simmer down.

Mama and me set about our buying. Papa and the older boys slowly walked toward a cluster of men and older boys.

The gypsies were gone but their wagon was still there, the horse gone, the banners and scarves and every other thing gone too, just the wagon husk there, something forgotten and unclaimed, untouched. I focused on a clump of wiry brown weeds caught against the closest wheel. If I looked at the wagon itself I would see something I didn't want to see or it would burst into flames. Or I would.

I wondered why they left their wagon behind. It was the only choice I allowed myself to consider. I saw them running away, perhaps the boy and his sisters on the horse, their papa and mama trotting on one side, one last glance at yet another town they never saw, that was what I made myself see, the boy high on the sturdy horse, one of those angel girls in front, the other behind, him putting one hand on his thigh, swiveling his shoulders and neck, his head turning, his eyes scanning for something to remember, to connect the words he'd heard, the faces he'd seen, that his sisters and mama and papa had heard and seen and felt, and the single girl who stood and listened and smiled.

Finally I closed my eyes and raised my head and when I opened my eyes the sky filled everything and I hunted the impossibly blue sky for fluttering black wings, a swipe of black.

But even as I searched, I knew no bird could show me what I wanted to see, I knew no matter how many times I swooped over all of Kansas I'd not see those gypsies again.

I meditated on what words would I have said to him, if I could relive that day, or what words if I saw him now, what first sounds under all the circumstances I could devise in my dreams.

1954

It was the year I went through all the Tom Swift books, senior and junior, and was into the Rick Brant series, which I liked better, Scotty the best sidekick a kid detective ever had. I was ripe for adventure—when I daydreamed, I saw myself as a grown detective stuck in a kid's body.

I looked for trouble everywhere. Followed people, grownups and other kids, if I thought they were suspicious or maybe just for practice, see how good I could be, stalking Main Street or the streets around school or where I lived, attaching myself to someone, skulking around behind trees and the corners of buildings, spying. I followed people to the IGA or the library, went in after them, trailed them through the aisles, saw to it they went home and not to some secret meeting.

I saw commie spies all the time. Or gangsters down from Kansas City. We'd all heard that Osawatomie had once been a favorite safe town for K.C. mobsters, a place where they could live away from where they worked. So there was plenty of cause to think I could see criminals lurking around town, needing to be watched, followed, kept track of.

That was my job. I didn't talk to anyone about it, not Jaimie or Woody or the twins. I knew no one would understand and I couldn't stand to listen to Lonnie's wisecracks. At least Brad would just roll his eyes or something equally theatrical, wouldn't go blabbing it all over. But Woody would, if for no other reason than to be the source of the juicy news. And Jaimie, well, Jaimie would just look at me like I was wasting my time doing something stupid.

From following just about anybody, it wasn't much of a leap to plastering myself to the Catholic kid, seeing what he was up to, see if I could find something out that no one else could.

He was harder to trail than I thought he would be. He walked fast, like someone on a mission, and didn't dally around. It excited me, thinking I was onto something.

He cut across Main Street and headed into the north part of town, the poor white part. I didn't know his neighborhood, had never really been there, except once to help pick up some newspapers for a Cub Scout drive, and I felt lost, even overwhelmed by all the unfamiliar places. I stayed back, maybe too far, scared I'd get caught, then get beat up. Like everyone else, I'd heard about juvenile delinquent gangs in this neighborhood so I kept my eyes open for ducktails and kids in Levi's with the bottoms rolled up in cuffs, showing engineer boots, shirt collars turned up; ready to hightail it out of there at the first sight of a J.D.

I didn't see any, but then I didn't see many people on the street period, like everyone was shut inside or something, watching TV or taking naps. It was eerie, ducking behind bushes and trees in yards where I'd never set foot before, peeking from around houses I didn't know, where dogs yapped from behind flimsy fences. But no one paid me any mind and I continued to follow the Catholic kid block after block.

He never looked back, never slowed, just walked, head up, pointed straight ahead like he was shot from a bow, someplace to be and he was late getting there.

He went to the Catholic church. First time I'd seen it, though I'd heard it was over here somewhere. Right away I saw it wasn't a cathedral, nothing like those pictures of Catholic churches you see in books. It was big, but not all that big, dark brick, stained-glass windows, a few crosses here and there. Some granite stonework around the front. Looked just like all the other churches in town, except the Presbyterian, which was some kind of off-white stone.

I was not going to follow him in. That didn't seem right plus I was sure I'd get caught in there. The priest would know on sight I wasn't a Catholic, he'd call the police or something. What was I doing there, a Methodist? I'd be in some kind of trouble, being in someone else's church, a place I didn't belong.

I watched a while, noticed the sun was going fast, and went home. What I'd learned was that the Catholic kid went to the Catholic church. Didn't seem like a whole lot to learn.

I followed the Catholic kid for two weeks after then, every day the same routine, a pell-mell walk to the Catholic church. He never wavered, beelining across town. It got so I didn't bother to hide much, stayed back, ready to hit the dirt behind a tree or a bush, rehearsed it in my mind as I walked along, saw myself launched horizontal, like Superman, rolling behind a shrub, crouching, waiting, watching. But he didn't stop, didn't look back, and I didn't dive into the bushes.

It got boring, his routine, so I stopped. I don't know what he did in there, each of those days. Maybe he was one of those choir boys, lighted candles or handed out little pieces of bread, I don't know. I couldn't quite see that, but what did I know about Catholic churches, what you had to do, your duties, to be Catholic, to save your soul.

Methodists didn't have to do much, I knew that. We went to Sunday school and church every week, took communion once a year, maybe twice. A mid-sermon snack, I thought. I wondered if Catholics got bored, doing it every week. Maybe it wasn't anything to get nervous about if you did it all the time.

I was pretty sure there was usually a lot of guys walking around at the front in a Catholic Church, all wearing long heavy robes in deep rich colors or maybe a stiff white. Embroidery, scallops, braiding. And the only other thing I knew was that there were all kinds of ways to do things wrong. I decided I was too nervous to be a Catholic. The added worry of all that additional sin would be too much.

I knew there was some other, bigger reason the Catholic kid was Catholic and that I was Methodist. I just didn't know what it was. I knew, however, that I felt lucky to be on my side of the difference, but, again, I didn't think I could explain it.

A year or two before, before Martha moved out near us west of town, she lived on Main Street west of downtown, and on days that I walked to Meek, I stopped at her house and she walked the remaining two blocks with me. Woody was with me some of the times, but mostly it was just me and Martha and we talked about school and our friends and who we didn't like. Martha wore dresses with petticoats, layers of white or baby pink fabric ringing her like frosting.

Then they built a new house and moved near my neighborhood but a couple streets north. They had money and a nice new rambling ranch-style house, with red siding and a long curving driveway that led to a two-car garage. No one else I knew had a two-car garage. Her house was no longer on the way to school, but by then I was riding mostly with a team of neighboring parents who'd set up a car pool.

Martha started inviting me over to her house after school, to play games, do homework, talk, eat snacks her mama set out, Oreo cookies and milk. About once a week, maybe a bit less than that.

One afternoon, about time the sun was setting, the light low and pink coming into her room through the west windows, we were sitting on her bed, talking. We sat a foot or so apart.

I want to tell you a secret, she said, but when I leaned toward her, turned my head, my ear ready to catch every word, she quickly kissed me twice on the cheek, giggled as she hopped off the bed and ran from the room.

I was startled, twice I'd fallen for that same trick. But I liked that she liked me and that she had kissed me.

She peeked back into the room, her face halfway visible around the frame. She had pretty black hair, dark eyes, intense expression, a gypsy girl.

I could see most of her smile and I was puzzled by how fragile it looked, as though the wrong sound would shatter it.

I made sure to smile back, tell her I liked that.

Still, at school we hardly said a word to each other, and in fact we went out of our way to be mean, loudly disdaining whatever the other said. It was expected, I guess, but it confused me, never really feeling that I knew which performance was the performance.

I believed in a kind of waking daydream I had two girlfriends. Martha had kissed me four times and asked me over a bunch. Sharon Marie gave me smiles only I saw. I didn't talk to anyone about either one, so it didn't matter how crazy I sounded to myself. I know some guys liked a particular girl, said nice things every now and then, or were caught waving or even talking, but I never heard anyone say they had a girlfriend. Did everyone have secret girlfriends, secret even from the girl herself?

I didn't know how this worked, I felt lost. But I know I enjoyed thinking about each one, and some nights when I sought dreams I tried to set in motion a picture story about me and Martha or me and Sharon Marie, grown up, married.

1960

John David

I could tell Woody wasn't too happy with how his night was going, had that sour look on full time. Woody's one of those guys got one of two ways when he was drinking. He'd either dance on the table tops, demanding everyone's attention, leading the way into the sloppy parts of the night, or, like tonight, go all quiet and turned inside, like instead of living it, he was reading about it on the inside of his head. He'd need some watching, because what was next, with him, was some down-and-dirty country mean.

He was giving me something to think about.

We careened a little along the sidewalk, Woody giving me the hairy eyeball, motioning with his head toward the theater.

Come on, he said, let's just do what we set out to do, John David.

Dorthea squealed, jokelike, then broke up into a kind of muffled giggle.

Oh, you boys wanna see some naked titties!

That okay with you? said Woody, stopping there, challenging her.

Sweetheart, she said, whatcha think I got under this here? She tugged at her dress. Her nails were extra long and painted the color of heart blood.

Nigger tits, said Woody, a mean smile stretched across his teeth. That's what I think you got in there.

Her smile got hard as dried clay and the twinkle disappeared from her eyes.

What's the matter with you, Woody? I asked.

Woody's look said he couldn't believe I didn't know the obvious. This look continued for a while. Something like the air that advances ahead of a thunderstorm seemed to hang over Woody. Cars passed. At the wheel, men with brim hats glanced at us, their passengers, wives or girlfriends, craned forward to catch a glimpse. Nothing was really going on but I felt like we were one or two words away from doing something that someone could sell tickets to see.

I didn't know what it was with him and Dorthea. I couldn't tell if it was simply disappointment about the burlesque or something else, or maybe that alone was enough. Talking about her that way, saying nigger, a word I could not myself use, except to tell about him using.

Woody, I said, then realized I had nothing to say. The words weren't there, just the feeling behind the words.

Ah, shit, he spit out, and he spun around, made a whole circle. Anyone just showing up would think he'd volunteered a dance for us.

Let's go, he said, and he started walking toward where we'd left his car.

Dorthea looked at me, eyebrows arched, and I shrugged. We tagged behind.

I wished I could say where we were headed, and I didn't mean out of town. I meant in the bigger sense. I was upset the way he'd been treating her, calling her a nigger and all, but that didn't fully explain what I felt that night. I was smart enough to know he was hurting, and that somehow he felt betrayed by my readiness to go along with the girl, but I didn't understand why it seemed to matter so much.

Or maybe I did. It had been on my mind from the beginning, how she reminded me of Sharon Marie, who'd been in the same class every year and we'd been friends and then she suddenly disappeared, moved away, her family gone to Kansas City, I heard. Five years ago, back when the railroad left and the town seemed to dry up. I still thought about her and was sure that's part of why I listened and went along.

1954

Milling around early a few days later, classes not starting for another thirty minutes or so. Standing on the walks in our familiar groups.

The twins came over, and we started idly wiping our shoes on the mud scraper. It hadn't rained for days and the only mud you'd find would be if you whipped it up yourself so all we did was scrape the bottoms of our shoes and make this uneven sandpaper sound.

Did you hear about the Catholic church? said Brad. He held onto the thick black bar and leaned back with his shoes on the scraper.

Yeah, said Lonnie, who stood straight and seemed more interested in what was going on up the block, toward where the three school buses were lined up, kids taking their time unloading, lots of chatter and milling around but nothing special that I could see. His foot rested motionless on the scraper.

What about it? I said. I rocked my foot back and forth on the edge of the scraper, my whole body rocking to some song in my head, something with a snappy beat. Hound Dog.

Someone set it on fire, said Brad.

Last night, said Lonnie.

Did it burn down?

Naw, said Brad. Just burned one corner.

It was some curtains or something and for some reason they didn't catch anything else on fire, just scorched the wall and burned up the curtains.

Got a pew, I heard, said Brad, looking at Lonnie.

I didn't hear that, said Lonnie, his tone saying that if he hadn't heard it was unlikely to have been said.

Do they know who did it? I asked.

I heard the Catholic kid did it, said Brad.

Me too, said Lonnie.

I watched the buses unload. About two dozen kids stood in clumps on the sidewalk near the front of the city library.

Why would he burn down his own church?

I heard he was angry at the nuns, said Lonnie. They beat him all the time. He caused trouble all the time, that's why he was sent there. He hadn't been in our classes for a couple weeks. I tried to picture him, tried to see him setting fire to a curtain. I could see it. I could see it just fine.

What are they going to do with him?

I don't know, said Brad. Maybe he didn't do it.

Or maybe they can't prove it, said Lonnie. Lonnie'd tell you, you listen, how he was going to be a lawyer. You could count on him to provide the legal angle.

You mean he hasn't been caught?

You mean arrested, said Lonnie.

I don't think so, said Brad. I don't know for sure.

I don't think he's in jail, said Lonnie.

Where would you hide in Osawatomie, where everyone knew everyone else. There weren't any caves or abandoned mines or badlands to get lost in. There was the park and the two blocks of downtown stores and the city golf course six miles out in the country and then all the farms that surrounded the town. But somehow I didn't see the Catholic kid hiding out in the country. Something about being Catholic made you a city kid; country kids were all Baptist or Methodist.

Maybe he ran off to Kansas City, I said.

Lonnie looked at me, curled his lip and squinted.

Why would he do that? he said.

Lonnie's disdain for this idea all by itself killed my conclusion that the Catholic kid had run off to the big city. Lonnie could spot a dumb idea faster and more accurately than anyone else although I thought he was sometimes a little stuffy about it.

I don't know, I said. Just an idea.

There's more Catholics up there, said Brad. To hide among.

Lonnie swiveled his attention to his brother.

Oh, you mean Father Flanagan might take him into the Home? said Lonnie. By the time he said 'Home' his voice sounded like a snarl.

You don't know, said Brad. Nobody does.

The Catholic kid does, I said.

Unless he didn't do it, said Lonnie. He may have disappeared because he's innocent but thinks everyone else thinks he's guilty.

I can see that, I said. I guess because it was true, we did think he was guilty; and had for years, it occurred to me then.

Who can we ask? said Lonnie. To make sure, get all the facts.

We each looked around while we thought on the problem, and it must have looked like we were scanning the area for someone with the answers. I saw Mrs. Friedman.

Hey, she might know, I said.

The twins saw where I was looking—at the couple steps up from the sidewalk to the short walk that led to the main steps, near where we stood—Mrs. Friedman, an armload of papers held against her chest and her eyes on the short set of steps, coming our way.

She's a teacher.

They looked at me.

They might've told her something since he used to be in her class, I dunno.

She was going to walk right by us, was only a dozen or so feet away. Her attention, though, was still downward, like she didn't want to trip over a crack in the sidewalk or something, she hadn't really noticed us.

Hi, Mrs. Friedman, I said. The twins said hello.

She looked up, her face seemed to snap into focus, and her mouth curled into her smile. Hello boys.

Can I ask you something?

Sure, she said.

Is the Catholic kid in some kind of trouble?

The Catholic kid? She looked confused.

Brad said his name.

Her look shot to Brad but all the confusion was gone, all the edges sharper, no longer blurred by doubts.

The fire at the Catholic church, said Lonnie. We heard he was in some kind of trouble about that. Is that true?

Why do you boys want to know?

Because we know him, I said.

He's your friend? she said. I don't remember you playing with him. I remember you staying as far away from him as you could.

We just want to know, said Brad.

I don't think there's anything for you to know, she said, put out at us, calling him the Catholic kid, I guess. Or talking about him starting fires.

You mean he didn't do it? asked Lonnie. He's innocent?

I have no idea what he did, she said. Or didn't do. Her face was stern. I was ready to bet she wished she had her ruler, could rap-a-tat-rap it on her leg. Or on one of us.

Well, we were just wondering, I said. We didn't mean anything.

She looked at me. I knew that look. From her, my Mama, all kinds of grownups: disappointment. It was something, as a kid, you got used to.

There are lots of other things you should be wondering about, she said. I will see you in class.

She hugged the papers to her tighter and climbed the steps, her head bent down a little, still looking for pennies or bad places on the steps or something.

We all looked at each other. Lonnie gave one of his superior smiles, although I wasn't sure quite why, what he'd thought had happened that made him look smart. It was just something he did.

The Catholic kid did it, said Brad. That proves it.

Lonnie's smile fell flat.

What? Lonnie and I said.

She didn't deny it, he said. Notice that? She dodged all around it. She knows something. She knows he did it.

So why didn't she tell us? said Lonnie.

Because we're kids, he said. Teachers aren't allowed to tell us anything that's real. You know that.

I watched Lonnie. I could tell he was thinking hard about that. I could tell it drove him nuts that his brother might be right, too.

That was when I told about following him those days, trailing him to the Catholic church.

You followed him? said Lonnie, amazed. Or, I think amazed. Maybe only dumbfounded.

I nodded, suddenly uncertain what to admit.

You tell anybody? Brad wanted to know.

You guys, I said, just now.

What an idiot, said Lonnie, shaking his head.

I hoped he meant the Catholic kid but I didn't feel very confident about my chances.

You see him start the fire? Brad, almost whispering it, like he was afraid just saying it somehow implicated him.

I don't think so, I said. I don't know. Maybe.

What's that mean? said Lonnie.

Yeah, said Brad. You saw or you didn't.

Some detective, said Lonnie.

Well, I said, attempting a tough look from TV. Lee Marvin. I saw him go in. Before.

Hours before, sounds like, said Lonnie, disgusted with me.

Brad smiled.

I don't think this was his first fire, either, I said, my voice a little louder than I'd intended.

The twins looked at each other, then me.

How about that fire killed Sharon Marie's cousin? I said. That one.

They looked at me.

He could've started that, I said.

You really don't like him, do you, said Lonnie, a smart-mouth smile growing.

Well, do you? I said back.

Brad shrugged. Lonnie just let his smile get bigger.

You read too many detective stories, John David, he said. Read some history books or something. Factual stuff. I think the Catholic kid's getting to you.

All day what everyone talked about was the fire at the Catholic church. Someone had set some drapes afire, spread up the drapes, scorched the wall there in the corner, and was just about at the ceiling when the priest, entering from a side vestibule, startled by the flames near him, yanked the burning drapes to the ground, stomped out the fire, burnt his feet and shins some, burnt the carpet where the drapes fell, the woodwork around where the floor met the walls, but nothing like it would have if the priest hadn't come along like he did, getting the fire out.

The next day was when I heard the Catholic kid had been arrested for the fire.

At recess, in groups, it was all you could hear.

FALL/1855

Simon needed watching. I knew that even though if you'd pressed me as to why I'd have been unable to answer other than he was ornery and never seemed to have the sense to figure things for himself.

He was the tool of the last person he spoke to, forever bringing home ideas from wherever he'd been. They weren't none of his ideas and about half the time he didn't know what he was saying, just mouthing words he'd heard, passing along gossip about things he had no knowledge of and if you asked him anything he'd shut up and blush and then either go off on some other tale that he figured somehow explained the first tale better—though it hardly ever did—or he'd get angry and accuse whoever was asking of not knowing nothing about anything.

He'd come home all excited, other people's words just spilling out of him like beans from a hole in his pocket and he'd wave his arms and shuffle and his eyes would be so big and bright that I sometimes feared they'd pop out of his head and roll off into some hole, be gone for good.

It was like the words themselves were his friends and he'd collect a whole new bunch as often as he could and bring them home to meet us. He admired his own stories, not because he was proud of what they were, but because he was the one who passed them along. The simple knowing and telling made him a part of the story which was generally an adventure.

You didn't have to be a full-grown man or woman to know that things were stirred up. It seemed like just about everyone's skin was on their faces a little tighter, their eyes quicker to dart around. It was a feeling that was so persistent you could almost hear it in the air, a song pitched so high you knew it was the voice of an injured angel.

Back in Tennessee we heard talk about Indians out on the plains, but it wasn't Indians got everyone skittering around. It was other white people, looked just like us so it was made doubly hard knowing who was the bad one and who was not. I think that's why people were more scared than if it was Indians making their days so miserable with fear.

Your own kind, it doesn't feel right.

But I knew we couldn't let them come along and take our land. We came here and walked this out, an honest walking, done it twice to make sure, and marked it with proper rock mounds, so that made it our land, and I knew Papa wouldn't leave. He came here to stop.

Free-staters lived on land all around us, land I heard had been taken away from ruffians that'd come over and staked out whole sections for the south. But they hadn't really wanted to stay and most didn't so the land was open, just floating here for anyone else.

We had one or two neighbors who'd come from southern states but we were generally outnumbered and like us they were here for the land, not the politics. It was the troublemakers, a small few, riled up feelings about our differences. Most of us just wanted to live our lives and work our land and get along.

Course, part of the problem was that at the moment we were blessed with two territorial governments, one recognizing abolitionists' land claims, the other the pro-slavers' claims. You could see how things were pointing to go. I knew of no claims against our land but that didn't mean one or two wouldn't show up one day like feral cats, ready to move in.

The trees had turned and all around us the hills and plains were dotted with the colors of fall. It was something to see in the sunset light.

Neighbor Wilkinson rode up to our place just before supper, a little hurry-up in his horse's steps, Wilkinson himself sitting stiff, bursting with something. We were all out front, everyone just used the well to clean up after the day.

Papa and William and Drury walked out a few steps to meet him, Simon edged himself tween them and me back under the doorway. Mama'd gone inside just a minute before, I could hear her making noises at Jonah.

The men all nodded at each other, Mr. Wilkinson touched his hat.

Could we offer you a drink of water, Mr. Wilkinson, Papa said.

That would be kind, he said, wiping his brow. It is warm today though I imagine we don't have many days like this left.

William caught Simon's eye and had him fetch Mr. Wilkinson his water, and he ran off like he was chasing a ball.

You heard that eastern abolitionist bastard's moved in over the hill, said Wilkinson.

No, I guess I have not, said Papa. William and Drury shook their heads.

Called John Brown, sometimes Old Brown. Been up in New York smuggling slaves into Canada, he said.

Runaways? asked Papa.

Yup. Mr. Wilkinson nodded his head toward the Lookout. He got a bunch of family been over there since spring, Staying with some in-laws, preacher Adair, them.

Papa nodded, so'd the boys. Simon joined.

I knew there was free-staters over there, said Papa. Hadn't heard about no famous abolitionist daddy though.

I heard he's full of fire and restless to put things into motion. A real tomcat, said Mr. Wilkinson.

Well, he'll fit right in around here, said Papa. We got no shortage of people with more opinions than sense. We got no slaves needs freeing around here. But I guess if you were setting a stage for some action, this would be a start.

I don't think his kind needs much in the way of facts to set their fuse. You have some trouble, you send one your boys over, me and mine'll come fast we can.

Mr. Wilkinson looked at Papa who looked at the sky for a thought or two before looking back at his neighbor.

Friend, we did not move our lives across the country to fight some war we got no part of. We do not wish you harm and we will help in every way but one. We will not get into a shooting war with people who live next to us. I do not expect trouble from people I share a fence with.

Mr. Wilkinson's face darkened, his posture sharpened, his mouth looked set like a knot.

I am sorry to hear that, sir. I hope the world finds a way to step around your place, he said, stopping, making a show of surveying our land. But I doubt if that will turn out to be the case, and he touched his hat and wheeled his horse around and set it pointed toward our gate.

Drury started walking in a circle, his arms flapping. William stared at him but Papa pretended not to notice, started to come back to the house. Supper was in the air.

Papa, Drury called out, his voice higher than he'd wanted. He said Papa again, not as loud, not as high-pitched. Papa, we can't do that, leave our neighbors helpless. That ain't right.

Papa stopped, the dust whirling around his boots. He turned back and faced Drury, who was still hopping around some, like he'd gone sleepwalking and ended up in the cooking coals.

And what's right? he asked. Is all us getting ourselves shot full of holes right? Is us joining up with some gang so we can kill some other bunch of men done joined another gang?

Papa, we can't run away.

We ain't running, Drury. We just ain't fighting no one while we're here. We are here to build our home and farm this land and that is what we will spend our time doing. You want to join some army and shoot at someone, go find a real one, but don't have nothing to do with no gangs of thugs and border trash.

Our property and preacher Adair's property, where all them Browns lived, shared a long common boundary exactly dividing the large mound that seemed to have been deposited from some other place, a miniature mountain in the middle of merely rolling hills. Everyone said that from its top you could see all the way into Missouri so everyone called it the Lookout.

It was where the two boys, our Simon and the Brown boy, Oliver, met, up there, the both of them just looking out over things, maybe hoping to sight some ruffians or Indians or something. Simon told me all about it, how they spent most of a too warm late fall afternoon skittering over the short-grass prairie telling each other tales about what they'd done and no doubt a few things they hadn't gotten around to doing but claimed on account of it was their due as young men on the cusp of manhood.

The only part of the tour around the edges of their neighboring property that later made Simon think that maybe this new boy wasn't the perfect new friend he could have been, was when Oliver at one point—perhaps the part where they'd accidently noisily flushed out a small pheasant that screeched and bashed the air loudly making its escape—paused and then pointed to where an abnormally thick stand of young white birch were themselves enveloped by thick green cat-tails: You could hide a dozen men with Sharps in there and control this entire area down through those ravines, his arm sweeping from the birch down along a nest of ravines to where they faded into the far low hills.

He looked at Simon as serious as if he'd been telling him the best way to skin a squirrel.

And why would you feel it necessary to do that, Simon asked.

You haven't been paying attention, have you? We're in a war. You could die today.

I don't feel that's too likely, said Simon.

Militia ride through this part of the territory every day, the Brown boy said. They shoot dumb boys like you for sport.

Simon said it was Dawson land, no one could come on it without our saying so, and sure couldn't start up no war that's for sure.

Is trouble scheduled for later this afternoon, Simon asked.

I've found that you can lessen trouble's surprise by being ready for it, the Brown boy said.

I understand preparation, Simon said. You ain't talking to no fool, but I don't understand the what-for here. We trekked across the Cumberland and Ohio valleys to get here, get away from the bully talkers asking other people to be good citizens, make the necessary sacrifice. I promise you the land, they said; I promise you bounty; I promise you a new world. We didn't come here to fight no war, we came to build something.

Well, you done took a wrong turn, I'd say, or you stopped too soon cause you ended up square in the middle of something that sure smells like war to me. My papa talks about it all the time. This is the time and this is the place. It starts here and it stops here, that's what he says.

Simon told me the Brown boy was practically shaking like he had the fever, his eyes full of purpose and someone else's blood.

Later, I would look back at that telling and say to myself it was when our brother was first infected with whatever it was that got into folks around here, when he first opened his eyes to things going on that were bigger than himself and bigger than us, and for that I never forgave the Brown boy because it was exactly the kind of thing we had tried to leave behind, or at least that was my impression, but then I was only a girl with nothing to concern me but my house duties. I was not permitted the kinds of dreams that dangled challenges larger than myself just out of reach.

Wasn't soon after Simon's supper talk grew wilder, him happy to pass along everything he heard. Or made up, was what William said to him after one fanciful tale about happenings in Lawrence and Westport and such.

In my opinion, Simon's biggest problem was the Brown boy, the way he put Simon under his spell or maybe he was only an excuse for Simon to bask in the heat from the boy's papa, the whole territory ablaze with news of Old John Brown moving here.

1954

Day or two later, in the middle of reading period, a little wad of paper bounced twice on my desktop and rolled into my lap. A note. I whipped my head around the room and saw nothing obvious. I'd missed the delivery. Two rows over one of the girls, Judy, smiled at me, but she smiled at everyone, all the time. Lonnie was rapt in a *Mad*, tucked behind his green reading book. Brad was trying to look up Mrs. Friedman's dress as she groped awkwardly beneath her desk for a pencil.

No candidates.

I unwrapped its folds, a line-ruled white flower blooming in my fingers.

JIMBOS DADDY BEAT UP HIS MOMMY BAD AND A MAN

All in blocky capitals, neither boy nor girl hints. I didn't recognize the handwriting. Jimbo. What the girls sometimes called Jaimie cause they think his name's supposed to be Jimmy. Girls can be dense beyond belief some days and mean more days than not or so it seemed to me.

I looked over at Jaimie. He was bent over the reading book slightly, his lips moving a little as he read. He wasn't the best reader in the room but he wasn't the worst either. Sometimes he stumbled on words I knew he knew, and when he did he'd stop and look up shyly and smile and then try again, his voice maybe a little softer. Some of the kids would snicker but not very many because almost everyone liked him and we all knew he wasn't a dummy.

He had that dreamy smile going as he read the words, his mouth curved up and his eyes a little too big for what he was doing. He didn't look like his daddy was in trouble for beating up his mama but who knew what that looked like.

It drove me a little crazy, wondering about what Jaimie's daddy had done and how Jaimie was doing, why he wasn't talking to me, why would anyone's daddy beat up their mama.

I tried to picture my daddy, wearing tan pants and a white T-shirt, neatly tucked in, his hair combed; and my mama, wearing shorts and a sleeveless blouse, and I could even almost see my daddy lean back and ready his fist, see his left arm extended, maybe grabbing or holding my mama, but I could not make the fist move forward, I could not remove my daddy's cockeyed smile or my mama's smile, could not imagine the punch at all, the picture freezes and then melts, and I wondered if Jaimie has tried to picture the same thing, or maybe he didn't have to, maybe he had a front-row seat, and I didn't know how to ask him which.

1855

Trouble filled the air like too many perfumed ladies in a small room, stifling and giving every thought or deed its own peculiar memory, the time when you could know things were going bad even before you heard about them.

Like battlefield rot, Papa said, although I hadn't known he'd ever seen a battlefield. But he often said things such as that and I always assigned it to the time when he was younger and was known to have read books.

Simon was our main source of news, due to his spending so much time with the Brown boy, since the Browns were either at the heart of the trouble or made it a point to know all about it. It filled Simon up to have all that news inside him and each day, it seemed, he burst with it, his face red and his eyes bigger than coat buttons, his hands waving away words as fast as he could spill them, and we sat in a circle and listened as quietly as if he was reciting the words of Jesus from the Bible. Mama and Papa even sat still for it although the looks that crossed between them as they heard the latest account of some free-stater's run-in with a ruffian were as loud as Simon's speechifying.

Papa had never cared for slavery, saying the slaves took good work away from white folk, and I know that was one of his reasons for leaving Tennessee. But surrounded here by so many free-staters and all their angry words, Papa felt he was being forced into choosing sides. Already Drury had joined the Kansas Law and Order Party. It was simply a matter of self-protection, he'd said, when Mama questioned him. William rolled his eyes.

We were not nigger lovers, that was for sure, and these days that left only the other choice and Drury embraced it with the enthusiasm he did everything. Papa soon doused some of his fire by declaring he didn't want to hear any of his talk, not at the dinner table, not while they shared work with him, not anywhere he had to listen to it.

There's enough damn things makes life hard without searching them out, Papa'd said. We came out here to live a life we could live and why all this nonsense is important I'll never understand.

Papa's goal was just getting through one winter and then another.

I went exploring one warm afternoon following lunch after first promising I'd be back in time to help Mama in the garden. I hiked east up the hill. I wandered over the crest and I just walked until I could see more than I'd seen since we'd left Tennessee, the Kansas territory rolling away from me in four directions. I could even see the smoke from some buildings down where Osawatomie must be; and our land; and our neighbor's cabin down and just a little to the east of where I stood.

Hey, whatcha doing up here, girl?

I spun around, startled, to see a boy about my own age just making his way onto the ridge from the north. I don't know why, but I hadn't seen him before that moment. He was dressed simple, just a pair of baggy coveralls and a clean gray work shirt, work boots, and a rough hat that hid most of his face in shadow.

I said, whatcha doing up here? This is Brown land.

I'm just looking. I meant no harm. I affected a frown. We own half this, I said. Other half's Adair land. Don't know no Browns, with land, that is.

He looked me over, his head moving just the slightest. He brought his hand up and picked something out of his teeth, then turned and spit.

They's blood, he said. My point, girl, is it ain't all just your land up here.

Even I could tell he was out of hot air.

You got a survey with you, points out which part you're standing on and which part I'm on?

I don't know what he saw or thought he saw but I wasn't much different, about the same height, our clothes from the same rough cloth, except I didn't wear a hat and my hair was long and auburn where his was short and darker. And I was a girl.

You're new here, ain't you, I said.

I been around for about sixteen years so I guess I ain't all that new.

He smiled, or at least I think he did, under the shadow of his hat.

You the family just move in down the hill?

He nodded. Name's Oliver. Oliver Brown. We're staying with my mama's people, till we get our own place going. That's our cabin there. But you know that, don't you?

My name's Sarah, I said, a smile lifting my face, surprising me.

He stepped closer and extended his hand. I'd never shook hands before. Men shook hands and no one had ever offered to shake my hand until then. I held out my hand and he took it, gave it a firm squeeze which I attempted to match and we pumped our joined hands up and down like milking cows.

Pleased to meet you, Sarah, he said, grinning.

Me too, I said, duplicating his grin. My inside wasn't happy with my outside, leaking smiles I wasn't sure I felt.

He spit into the dirt again and he turned his face, looked off toward where our land was.

You're our neighbors, he said. It wasn't a question.

It's a big territory, I said, wondering a little what I'd meant by that. There seemed to be some point needed making.

He returned his gaze to me.

Why'd your people move here?

My Papa heard the land was good, I said. And we weren't doing so good back in Tennessee.

I remembered the last two winters there when we'd eaten hardly anything but potato stew with sometimes a piece of game thrown in, if my Papa could bring down a deer, which seemed less and less easy to find as people shoved the animals aside for their farms.

We're here to fight slavery, he said, his voice taking on something new, had a preachy note to it. My daddy's dedicated to it.

Far as I know, they ain't no slaves round here, I said.

We aim to keep it that way, he said.

This was the leading topic of just about any conversation among men but mostly no one had asked me what I thought.

What I could tell, his eyes shaded under that hat bored into mine. The boy had heat pouring out of him like someone had spilled coals in him and the only way the steam could get out was through his glowing eyes.

Niggers is all anyone talks about, I said. That and northerners coming in here to fill out the vote for statehood. Where I come from there's slaves and it's given a white man is plain better than a nigger.

His look was so hard I thought for a moment that he would turn and stalk away.

Maybe there's things about people you just haven't considered, he said. You should think on that.

He looked at me, stony.

You're a girl, you're supposed to be smarter than that, he said.

Which plain shut me up.

What if you'd been stolen and taken to Africa and made a slave, your family broken up, all your choices removed, yourself not allowed to be yourself, nothing you did was yours to do?

That is a stupid question, sir, I said. I ain't in Africa and no nigger'd be up to taking me there. Your imagination is too big for your britches, dreaming up such a thing. How can I take you seriously, you talking about sending white people to Africa?

No man should own another man, simple as that, he said. There just ain't no more to be said on the subject.

He shook his head, spat one more time, and then turned and walked away, got twenty, thirty feet off and turned back.

You need to get back to your people, he said. This ain't gonna be no place for you.

1954

I heard you been talking about me.

I turned, saw the Catholic kid standing there. The second thing I noticed was that his hands were balled into fists, trembling at his side. And then I noticed that he wasn't as much bigger than me as I'd thought. That surprised me.

Whatcha mean? I said.

You know, he said, his voice husky with emotion. You been saying things about me, I'm some kind of baby killer.

I never said that, I lied, although I told myself it was not a lie: I'd never said he was a baby killer. But I had said I'd heard—from whom? no one; I'd put it together on my own—that he'd started some fires and that one fire had killed Sharon Marie's baby cousin.

I ain't never killed no baby, he said, his lower lip matching the beat of his fists.

Okay, I said, good enough for me.

I started to turn away, hope he'd go away.

I said I ain't never killed no baby, he repeated. You hear me?

His voice louder now. I think he'd moved closer, though I hadn't noticed him move at all.

I backed away a step, maybe two.

You got to take it back, he said.

I looked at him, wondering how I could do such a thing. Go around, tell kids he hadn't killed Sharon Marie's cousin.

Okay, I said.

He stared at me, thinking about what to say or do next. I could tell he was considering more than one thing. Hitting me was right up there near the top of the short list.

And I didn't start no fires, either, he said, but his voice was less forceful.

Okay, I said.

You stop talking about me, he said.

Okay.

Okay, he said.

He gave me an odd look, his eyes narrowing, his mouth scrunched, but somehow I knew it wasn't real, it was some kind of act. The danger point had passed. I would not get beat up.

He backed away a step and then turned and walked away. It was then that I noticed we'd had an audience: Jaimie, Martha, Woody, the twins. And back a few more steps, Sharon Marie, her arms tight around some books, her eyes round, reflecting something I'd never seen before: a heartbreaking combination of horror and disappointment.

I'd let her down. It had been my moment to bring out into the open what we all suspected, and I'd failed the test. In fact, I knew, I'd failed more than one test.

We looked at each other, forgetting the others, just the two of us, fifteen feet apart, friends since kindergarten, the only girl I ever said anything of consequence to, who always had something nice to say to me. Who I dreamed about and never told anyone, hardly myself.

And then another thought came to me as we looked into each other's eyes. She hadn't wanted to hear any part of what she'd heard. She hadn't wanted that new suspicion or doubt or whatever it was. It was awful enough when all it was was a terrible accident. It was too much to bear to believe anything worse.

There it was, scratched into my head like in some old cave, I was always going to disappoint Sharon Marie, I was missing what it took to not do the wrong thing. I wasn't brave enough for her.

I couldn't stand it no more, I broke off looking at her, the pain and confusion simply too much for my heart to bear. But then I gave myself a little speech in my head, told myself something more important than my feelings was at stake and I looked back up at her but she'd turned and was walking away, one foot slowly in front of the other, her head angled down just the slightest bit.

And I kept my mouth shut and watched her walk away, knowing I'd allowed something to change that wasn't something I wanted changed.

1960

Woody

S he'd thrown some kind of spell on John David, that much was clear. But I just gave up fighting him about it and we headed back to my car. It was still there, at least that part had gone right, and soon we were bunched inside, the nigger in back, John David in shotgun where he belonged, and we was winding our way through the streets of Kansas City, the nigger suggesting ways to go and me telling her to stow it, I knew my way, and John David casting looks back and forth from me to her.

I got a little turned around but no one said anything and after a short detour I found U.S. 50 and was pointed back south. I still didn't get why we were taking her to Osawatomie.

Remind me, I said, just why are we taking you with us?

Her brother's money, I think she said, answered John David.

Why, honey, it's such a nice night and I ain't never been to Oh-sa-wot-o-me, she said, going for that movie star voice, sing-songy and playful, but I knew better, none a her tricks would work on me. We weren't never about to be best friends.

You know about Osawatomie? I asked.

Well, she said, I do, I surely do, still doing that stupid voice.

John David turned around, looked at her.

Yeah? he said, all friendly like, encouraging. What do you know? Getting real interested, like she was gonna prove to be some undiscovered Einstein.

It's where my brother's money is at, she said, proud as can be.

I could just about hear John David's smile break into little pieces, even with the windows down and all. I knew they both heard me burst a laugh.

We were on a mission to retrieve some nigger's money, get him out of jail. Ain't that just a kick, I thought. Wait'll I tell about this one.

It was a mistake, asking about her brother because she threw herself into a long nigger story about how they grew up, all their bad luck being niggers and all, getting so wound up she demanded to sit with us, and John David made me pull over so she could squeeze into the front seat.

I could feel her all along my right side and her smell was in every breath I took, even with all that air blowing by. There was a kind of heat coming off her enough for two people, like inside her dark skin was twice something.

The road stretched out ahead, rushing white lines, the white head-light cone pushing into the night, the nigger girl's heat taking over my head.

The first time the car caught fire, we were a little ways north of Olathe, the lights of Kansas City still glowing bright in the rear-view mirror. John David had been twiddling with the radio for about five minutes, finally settling on some nigger station way over at the end, some blurry-sounding bunk, but it seemed to make the nigger girl all cheery and at least I didn't have to listen to her talk about her no-good brother.

We'd picked up some more beer on our way out of town so I wasn't as angry as I had been. I didn't know about finding some nigger's money but I knew I was heading home and when we got there I was gonna turn this whole adventure over to John David, let him sort things out. I was gonna be done with it. And I was gonna let him do it without a car, too, see how that put the polish on his apple.

What's that smell, said the nigger.

What smell, I said, not saying what I wanted about what might be smelling up my car.

John David leaned forward and looked at me, then at the girl, wrinkled his nose a few times, looked back at me.

Something's burning, Woody, he said, bending down to get his face near the floor vent.

I caught a few whiffs of something, that acidy electrical odor like when you got too many things plugged into some outlet.

John David reached up, switched on the dome light and we saw right off some graylike smoke drifting up from the vent.

Shit, I think we're on fire, said John David. You better pull over.

1954

The new roller rink sat on the corner facing the railroad tracks a vacant lot away. The whole thing unpainted cinderblock, flat roof, windowless, the entrance at the corner nearest the street and the tracks, double swinging doors under a red curved awning. Inside, the counter where you rented skates, a changing area, and the rink, a large wooden floor with a double rail-wood fence around its perimeter, a walkway behind that, around the rink, some benches here and there. A concession stand.

It was Martha's birthday party and all of us had the rink to ourselves up until a certain time when the older teenagers could take it over. The rink was awash in swirling reds and oranges and yellows, greens, blues, and someone was playing 45s over the sound system so we circled to Buddy Holly and Elvis Presley and Wanda Jackson, but the Bunny Hop was still the Bunny Hop.

I knew how to skate pretty good since learning on the concrete streets around where we lived, used the kind that clamped on around the toes and a strap across the ankle, had little square keys to adjust them, and you wore the key on a string around your neck where it swayed steady as a metronome if you did it right.

This smooth surface combined with the skates-on-boots, and it was grand gliding around the floor, crossing one leg languidly over the other as I swooped through slower traffic like a Sabre jet on the hunt.

Martha was there, of course, and the twins, and Woody. Bobby. Bruce, Mike, Dina, Janice, Darlene, and just about everyone else.

We were all dressed a little better than we would be for school but nothing as severe as Sunday best: nice jeans, sweaters, bright shirts buttoned to the neck, belts through every loop, and plenty of Brylcreem, our do's glistening under the revolving colored lights.

I skated a dozen revolutions with Martha, even let her hold my hand as I led her through the maze of other skaters, but then she let go after a couple circuits and we slowed and skated side by side for a while before she angled into the rest area. She turned her head as she started to veer away, her eyes dark and big; a half-hearted smile flickered, didn't catch, and faded to something else and then she was gone, her back to me, her long hair swaying to the beat.

There was something about Martha's look that felt like it had thrown a switch, and something I hadn't known I now knew but I was still disadvantaged by not having a name for it.

I saw myself skating around the rink with her, the half gloom and the swirling lights turning everyone the same twinkling colors. She was as light as tissue.

I snapped to and looked around at Martha's party. I looked at only a few faces before I acknowledged I was looking for Sharon Marie. She wasn't there. Or Jaimie, or any of the other colored kids. But it was Sharon Marie I looked for, even expected to see, and I scanned the faces, saw they were all white, said to myself, none of them are here, and I stared at each face, asking myself what I had meant, why I had looked for her skin and not her. I questioned myself. A place near my heart compressed and ached. Everything I learned any more hurt; getting older didn't solve things, it only added on new things to solve.

I made myself dizzy spinning out sentences in my head that explained what I saw—all the white faces reflecting the dancing lights, the mess of colors, and in my mind our missing classmates. It seemed like a club had formed and it didn't include all the ones it should.

I looked at my bare arm, its bone whiteness with the fine hairs that I hated. I squinted my eyes almost shut and saw my arm go fuzzy and dim, a darkness almost like colored skin. I didn't feel any different, it was still an arm. I wondered what it was I didn't understand, what was the thing that made a difference that mattered. I didn't understand how this made any of us right or wrong or why that was even part of the question.

* * *

Later, Woody and I think Bobby and me started fooling around, zooming around in a strung-out pack, like segments of a high-speed snake, articulating, flowing, cutting, and, okay, maybe jostling some of the other skaters, the real slow ones or the ones who didn't yield. We passed and repassed each other, each of us bent over at the waist, our arms pumping, our legs scissoring.

Until the Catholic kid stuck out his foot and caught Woody's right ankle just as he started his glide, sent him tumbling into a line of three pokey girl skaters, skirts stuffed with petticoats arced over as Woody and the three rolled to a stop against the sideboard. Behind him, the rest of us went down, four spinning tops taking everyone we touched until we spun down to nothing.

The music stopped. The PA crackled. The lights flared up. All the colored lights were gone or muted to almost all white.

We'll have none of that speed skating or you will be kicked out. Is that clear? boomed the PA voice.

No one said anything. I wasn't sure who he was talking to, anyway. The Catholic kid went by, his smirk about a twinkle away from bursting into loud laughter.

Against the boards, the three girls were swatting at Woody who was trying to disentangle himself from their limbs and what looked like several rolls of creamy fabric. He had his arms over his head as he tried to get away. One of the girls was squealing.

He touched me! He touched me! she cried. Her eyes were huge and she waved a finger at Woody, who had stopped a safe distance away and was looking at the girl. His eyebrows were arched and his mouth gaped; he looked confused. Maybe he'd hurt himself when he fell.

He didn't hurt you, Janice, I said. Be quiet about it. Nothing happened to you.

He touched me, she said, and he shouldna.

He fell, Janice, and crashed into you. That wasn't a touch, that was a tackle.

Her friend Darlene leaned in close to Janice and held her closed hand in front of their mouths as they exchanged heated whispers.

Okay, okay, Janice said, and she rose, used the nearby railing to pull herself to her feet where she was joined by Darlene and they set to dusting off each other's billowing skirts. Janice made a show of her unhappiness, her mouth so deeply drooped that her lips made the letter n and her gestures were exaggerated, her moans a little too loud. Darlene continued to whisper seriously and slash at the dusty skirts.

Don't think you can come in here and get away with that kind of behavior, young man!

I spun around at the first word and there stood the rink owner, Mr. Russo. He wasn't very tall but he was huge, all head and neck and chest, arms, buttocks, and legs, everything extra thick. He walked funny, had one of those back-and-forth waddles, all his movement coming from his hips, his knees hardly flexing at all; it was the way robots walked in the science fiction movies. And I'd heard that he was connected to the rackets or something. He was sneaky. I knew quite a lot of parents hadn't wanted the roller rink because they knew who the owner was and they just figured it would become a hangout for criminals or at least J.D.s.

What saved me was he was an adult and I had yet to talk back to grownups so I lowered my eyes and said I was sorry and I wouldn't do it again. No one was kicked out.

Someone later told me the Catholic kid had sneaked in, that's how he was there. Everyone knew it anyway, knew Martha wouldn't have asked him.

WINTER/1856

D ark clouds pressed down on the sleek black bird as it glided and rose over a hillock. Below, tucked away under a stand of bare black oak, three horsemen, huddled, leaning up on their saddles, focused on the roadway, which snaked around rock and water and ravines, scars on the weaving green-brown floor.

They grew smaller the higher the bird soared, then spinning down a long glassy slope cutting the curving road straight, flashing over a lone rider, pushing his mount a little more than a walk, in a hurry but a long way to go, the rider's legs tense, his back too straight, his head swiveling. And up with a draft, keeling, diving back down the road to where the three were, waiting, now seeing the rider and leaning back, behind the branches, behind the rock, two pulling Sharps rifles from leather scabbards, the other drawing a pistol, exchanging looks, nodding heads, the horses noticing the difference, their heads coming up, their ears alert, shaking their heads, clouds of steam billowing out of their noses, one stomping a foot, its rider leaning over and whispering into its ear, patting its damp flank, the rifle pointed up like a flag.

Then they slapped their horses and wheeled around the trees, charged into the roadway, stopped in a swirl of red dust, the lone rider yanking on his horse hard, calling out, whoa, steady steady! The horse danced nervously, up and to the side, flicking and shaking its head, nostrils flaring, its breath tumbling out white, wet snorts.

And you be steady, sir, said the one with the pistol, loosely pointed at the ground.

Let me by.

We got a question for you. We was wondering if you'd be one of them free-staters? He gripped the pistol tighter, the barrel lifted a ways.

He smiled, lips tight across his teeth, eyes unmoving, brows lifted so every bit of light'd get in.

The rider allowed his horse to continue to hop, still spooked, it looked natural enough then when the horse made a half circle, the rider's gun hand hidden, and then when he spun back around, he brought to bear a long barrel forty-four revolver, held steady on the man whose own pistol was frozen aimed at a wild rose.

The rider leaned forward and said something to the horse without moving his eyes from the bunch in front of him, soothed the horse, everything settling down, the rider's big handgun solid as a thick tree branch.

What I believe about anything ain't none your business, he said. Now move aside and let me pass or I will start putting holes in you.

The two horsemen with the rifles frowned, one glancing at the man holding the pistol, who shook his head like he'd come home and learned his baby boy had been playing with the axe.

There are three of us, in case you don't know your 'rithmetic, he said. You ain't gonna do nothing we don't do to you worse.

Maybe you kill me, the rider said, maybe you don't but I guarantee I will put a hole in you big enough to hide a cat. Hell, mister, them other two don't even have they rifles cocked so I figure I'll get at least two of you before the last one finds the trigger. I like my odds—how you like yours?

This ain't good, Oden, said one with a Sharps.

Shut up, said the pistol holder. He stared at the gun barrel pointed directly at his chest, unwavering.

He released the hammer on his cocked pistol with his thumb, let the barrel drop straight down, and smiled wistfully at the rider, whose expression was grim and unchanged.

Okay, mister, today you was lucky, but we will see you again and next time I will just straight out shoot your horse and then you.

Sure you will, said the rider. Get your yellow asses back to Missouri. Your mamas calling you. He held steady until the three men had wheeled around and walked their horses back up the road, east.

After a few hundred feet, one raised his eyes and watched the birds dotting the pale sky like spilt peppercorns, then he turned in his saddle and looked back, the rider out of sight, but he was pretty sure he was back there, behind that tree or that rock, watching them recede into the horizon.

Wesson got himself stopped other afternoon, said William. Three of them, the road from Dutch Henry's Crossing.

Simon snapped around, hopped over to where William sat in Papa's rocking chair, you'd thought he was giving out treats. He lost some years of maturity in my heart, way he puppy-dogged over some things.

Who were they? Did Wesson shoot any, asked Simon.

William stilled the rocker and looked at Simon.

This is not the gypsies here to entertain you, William said. He claims they were Missouri border trash and just assumed he was some free-stater. I guess they never got around to sharing their politics, it was just these rundown farm boys pointing guns and then Wesson pointing his and no one volunteering to be the one to start the whole mess.

Wesson said they weren't the brightest bunch.

Drury turned to William, looked like he had something to say. We mighta seen those men, those three we saw on the crest road when we was clearing the low piece, he asked Simon.

Yeah, they didn't look right. We were way down and mostly hid by brush and them backlit up on the road. They seemed real focused on where they was going like folks do when they're passing through, letting you know they ain't interested in you or your things.

Simon beamed.

Well, we know better than that, I guess, said William. Round here everyone seems interested in everyone else's business. I never seen anything like it, both sides preaching freedom of one kind or another but then they won't let each other alone. And then folks shoot each other cause they feel slighted or put out.

Well, if it was sense you were looking for, brother, you started with the wrong topic, said Drury. You want a bunch of free niggers your neighbors, he said, leaning forward like he'd stepped outside and there was a big wind coming over the plains right into his face.

You mean they'd be worse than the trash we got to deal with now, William said quietly, more quiet than I'd have thought considering Drury's fire.

I can't believe I'm hearing you say something like that, Drury said. They's ain't like us and you can't tell me different.

Hell, Drury, the whole world's different, you pay any attention. You're different from sister Sarah—you want just men in the world, that what you're saying? Just how you slicing it, brother? What parts you want different or the same?

Your fancy talk ain't gonna argue against what I can see with my eyes, what any damn fool can see. They's niggers and we are white and you ain't gonna tell me you can't see that.

I ain't arguing you can't tell a difference, I'm only asking you to tell me what it matters. You gonna do less work because you got niggers over the next hill? You gonna forget your upbringing and revert to something you can't even name? What in your mind is gonna happen you end up sharing the world with niggers?

Drury closed up his face like someone slapping shut a book, leaned himself back, almost like he was trying to push himself back through the chair. His hands gripped the chair, his knuckles pale as flour dust.

He cut me a glance, his mouth opened then he shut it, gave me another look, hissed, You know what's gonna happen, you just don't want to say it. Him looking at me again.

William, you want me to leave the room so you can tell our brother what a jackass he is, I said.

You do not know the ways of the world, Sarah, said Drury. You simply have no notion.

I have more of a grasp of the world than you know. Who do you think picks up your men's mess? Who has to make do when something catches your attention? And if you are talking about rape, I said, my eyes level and unblinking, then just who exactly knows better its costs than the woman? You are full of romance. It is you who needs to take stock of the world. I see it just fine.

There was no more said that night. Little sister had surprised them, snipped at the extended hand. It was my hope that at least one of them considered my persuasion and tried to understand my true self.

1954

Jaimie's attendance started to vary—I don't believe he went every day a whole week all winter. It saddened me on mornings when the last bell rang and his desk remained empty.

Where's your girlfriend? the Catholic kid sneered, twisted around in his desk, catching me looking at Jaimie's seat folded up.

My girlfriend? My mind snapped on Martha and Sharon Marie. I tried to remember what the Catholic kid could know about what, his question only about then becoming clear to me.

You're funny, I said. But not as funny as you look.

My pops calls your kind nigger lovers, he said, his voice lowered.

All the negroes I know are better than you, I said. But then so's my dog's brown butt.

Before the last word cleared my mouth he'd launched himself down the aisle, grabbed my shirt, yanked me out of my desk, then together we toppled to the floor, rolled entangled, banged into other desks, distant voices screaming, feet scrambling away from us, him growling and snorting, his eyes wide wide open, and then his hands letting go and then a rain of fists fell on my head, all around my face, and I squeezed my eyes shut and tried to get my hands up in front of my face but his arms, moving like machine parts, kept knocking my arms aside. I couldn't seem to cover myself, and I started to come undone, I just couldn't stand it, the top of my head was throbbing with his punches, my whole face stung, and I exploded, every muscle convulsed and I bucked like a wild bronco, tossing the Catholic kid up and over, his head catching the edge of Woody's desk, a sound like a stick snapping, and the Catholic kid crumbling, his eyes staring at me, the strangest look of surprise, like a question just starting to form, his red fingers twitching against the worn wood floor.

Mrs. Friedman was there, bending over the Catholic kid, whispering a single word, Bruce?

The Catholic kid said nothing, did nothing, except his fingers, tapping.

He attacked me, I said.

Yes, yes, John David, I know, but let's not talk about that now. I've got to take care of Bruce, she said, kneeling down next to him, a hand stroking his head.

He didn't die but he got taken to the hospital, siren dying as the ambulance sped away from school, everyone looking at me and then no one looking at me, pointed at or ignored, seemingly both happening at once. I was confused, didn't know whether to move quietly to the coat hall or sit down and wait for someone to say something to me or the police to take me away, put me in jail. I tried to figure what was going to happen but my pictures of the future trailed off into gray mystery, nothing and everything made sense, it was the end of something and the beginning of something.

Mama found me in the coat hall, sitting under the coats, knees drawn up, shivering from something that felt like a fever but wasn't.

John David, what happened? She knelt beside me.

The Catholic kid jumped on me and beat me up and I threw him off and he hit his head and a doctor came and they took him to the hospital, I said.

How did it start?

He called me a nigger lover so I said he was funny looking and that was when he jumped me.

Mama looked at me, then looked at the wall for a minute, then back at the door, and then back to me. Her mouth made the funniest smile but her eyes glistened and clouded.

You didn't do anything wrong, she said.

And then I cried and she put her arms around me and we were like that for a while and then we went home after Mama talked with Mrs. Friedman and old Mrs. Mullins, the principal.

1855

I don't know why I called the Brown boy the Brown boy and not thought of him by his name Oliver, which I knew because he believed it necessary to introduce himself first few times I saw him, him acting in part like he was first meeting me, even his smile had that slightly awkward tilt that almost always meant embarrassment or humiliation or hurt was just under the surface and you knowing your first words could wield the knife he feared his hello would generate.

But I never let him off that easy, that smile signaling to me he could be playing a role, get one over on the girl, for whatever reason though of course I had my own ideas about that; for one, my own feelings were roused, in both the obvious physical way—he was clearly a handsome boy, even a kind of fragile prettiness I am sure he knew about and maybe even hated but took advantage of—and also because he confounded and astounded me the way a puzzle expands what can be envisioned, dangling hints and possibilities like Christmas ornaments, sending diamonds of light dancing across my face until they coalesced into a language I could understand.

It must have occurred to him after about the second or third meeting that he could not continue to act as though we were first meeting, that road had done run straight into the wall, and he must have realized that his artifice would be apparent to me, and that I would wonder exactly how dumb was he anyway.

I knew he'd either continue to behave like a boy or recognize his mistake and drop his games and devices and talk to me. And I knew he'd do this without mentioning his previous behavior. He would simply be a different person one day.

* * *

I am telling you, our brother, sin is something you agree to, swear to, believe in, but it isn't part of the natural world which is as it is in whatever way that is, without judgment or point of view. What is done, what happens in the natural world are the things themselves without merit outside themselves or perhaps in the eye of their beholders but the point is there isn't any sin involved. What one thing does to another is merely its nature, and how are we outside that, our brother, how are we the exceptions to all that is the world, every living god-created thing?

We are special, he said. We are given speech and a brain.

Oh, darnation, Simon, every darn thing has a brain. And you know from watching and listening that there's things being said by just about everything, birds and coyotes and dogs and anything that makes a noise or winks or scratches in the dirt. How do we know what they know, what they can do.

Cause we're smarter. We build things.

I'm not sure we're smarter, our brother. We sure seem to make messes from things. Take a perfectly fine country like this is and confuse people's priorities with politics; we should all be putting our attention on our fields and crops and animals.

It got so hardly anyone talked to me, I was so riled from sunrise to sunset, and the way my bedding looked in the morning, I must have taken being riled to fulltime. Which set me to wondering, as I did, why nothing about things seemed right to me, I was always taking them apart and though I said it was just to talk about, to look at closer, everyone but me sensed my anger and I was given wide berth, and soon I was telling the cow how to make milk and the chickens their eggs were on the small side.

1954

The Catholic kid didn't come back to school. He couldn't move his arms and legs. I'd made him a cripple. No one knew what to say to me, their eyes serious, words squeezed out like mud between fingers of a closed fist. And I didn't know what to say back, nothing that came to mind sounded right, it all sounded like the kind of excuse I'd give Mama when I'd done something I knew was wrong and didn't want to get in trouble, but this time Mama kept saying I hadn't done nothing wrong, it was just one of those things that happened when something tumbled out of control, like when you spun a top and it went where it went, bounced off stuff and you just never knew where it'd end up, what it might break.

But I didn't feel like it was a spinning top that careened from chair leg to table leg. The Catholic kid was stuck in a bed in a hospital and the only thing he could move was his head. Someone told me he never said anything about me, but I didn't really believe that, as much as I wanted to. I could not accept he didn't have a lifetime of words lined up, all aimed at me like poisoned arrows.

Soon after, I was in the front room, in the big chair by the window, rocking, reading a Batman comic, Mama called my name, almost a loud whisper. I looked up and saw her at the head of the hall, leaning into the room, one hand on the wall, her other beckoning me, come here, her hand said.

I followed her back down the hall to their room and when we were there Mama said, shut the door, and I did, not making much noise because that was how it felt, like something secret was going on.

I want to show you something, she said, squatting in front of their chest of drawers, the big, black hunk of wood with eight wide drawers.

Do you know whose this is, she asked, her left arm draped over the top of the chest of drawers. Do you?

No, I said.

It was Mother Dawson's, given her by her mama. It's been in the family since forever, she said. Let me show you something. Help me pull it away from the wall a little, okay?

She showed me what she wanted me to do and we pulled together and moved the chest away from the wall and she said, look, here, take this and shine it on the back there and tell me what you see.

She handed me the flashlight and I clicked it on and pointed it in the angled space, filled it up with blue red light and saw carved into the dull black wood were two sets of initials separated by a plus sign, boyfriend girlfriend, I'd seen it on countless notes winged around school, here SD+OB.

That's Mother Dawson, Sarah, and the Brown boy, Oliver. He went off with his daddy to Virginia to start a slave rebellion. He had a thousand spears tucked away in a farmhouse up from Harper's Ferry ready to hand out to the slaves that he envisioned would join him. They never got married, but she had a baby and that baby was your great-greatgranddaddy Simon Oliver and he married and his only daughter Elizabeth married an Oldfather and it all leads to me and then to you. We are Browns, John David, although no one around here will say so. It is something that only we know.

I didn't know what to do with this news, what it meant.

The other thing is, John David, we've got to be careful, because Browns can get carried away with some funny notions and set out to do something the exact wrong way.

1856

That odd blue light that beams off a full moon kept me awake one night, filling up the house bright enough to read by, and after tossing and turning enough to get my heat up, I surrendered to the strange light and got up and threw a shawl over my nightshirt and stepped outside where the air billowed out the plain cotton and cooled me instantly.

Something pulled me away from the house. Some noise or persistent thought had sent me outside, the moon fat overhead, that familiar midnight insect buzz, the sky alight with stars.

Something like a whisper had been at me all night.

And off to the side, a movement, something large and not very fast but gone from sight, one dark gray shape melted into another, out by the small shed.

Unafraid for some reason, I stepped off the narrow porch and strode purposefully toward the shed, where Papa kept some of his tillers, the busted ones, and some other tools.

A noise slowed me, so I could hear better, and there, again, the night dark grays dancing just out of my direct sight, but I heard breathing familiar from all the time I'd spent spying on him, indirectly.

The Brown boy was out there, maybe here to see Simon or even entice him to join him and his brothers and Old Brown in some kind of crazy stunt we'd all be reading about in the free-state newspapers and talking about for months; or maybe be plainly killed, the random meeting in one place of a lead ball and Simon's foolish head.

He never came over to just visit or anything. His earnestness made me think he strained under the burden of having such a crazy and famous papa. I knew daddies were hard to please, but if about the only thing your papa respected was killing slavers, then it was pretty obvious what your course of action had to be. And I thought everyone knew, at least in their hearts, that killing was a line that once crossed could not be undone; it was a new and permanent way to look at yourself and it would never get any better.

I would not say I knew the boy at all, just that time up on the Lookout and then a few words here and there, everything else I knew I knew from watching. I knew his philosophy well enough without bothering myself with more wasted talk. But the fact he was a Brown shaded every facet of him. His eyes, though perhaps merely brown, took on different shades knowing what they had seen. His mouth could have been merely slack at times but to my eyes it looked cruel. I fought with my heart over this, because I knew it was wrong to judge someone without the proper facts, but my feelings were so strong I gave in. I'm not sure listening so intently to my heart can be finally called a weakness, but I was raised up to believe in people until they gave you reason not to.

A breeze rustled the leaves and brought me awake, as though I had been sleepwalking and hadn't known how I'd gotten out here, though of course I had done nothing of the kind and remembered clearly awakening. But what, after all, was I doing out here, I could not answer.

Simon was inside, asleep. I could not be watching after him. I was here for some other reason. Some other curiosity.

A snap drew my eyes back toward the edge of the shed where I believe a shadow had detached itself from the dark and was now moving away from the little building.

I called out, not loudly, and the shadow stopped, like the wind suddenly disappearing and a billowing sheet going limp on the clothesline.

My eyes attempted to focus on the shadow and the dark played tricks, made it grow larger, darker, and when I cut my eyes away, to the side, it paled some, shifted back to its smaller size. It was now a frozen shape, unmoving, even in the wind, which continued to rise and fall like breathing.

I called again.

A trick of light and dark and there he was, larger, darker, only a few feet away.

What do you want, he said. Why are you out here?

I think that is my question, I said. Maybe you are lost and don't recall who lives where.

His face slowly took on features as my eyes adjusted. I saw the pale light curve of his white teeth.

Though he was slight, like all young men, he had a weight about him, like he was the center of things and planets circled him.

A powerful feeling took hold of me, I had no words for it, but as clear as knowing two and two add to four I knew I wanted to hit him or kiss him, and this feeling filled me up like sand. Inside, my heart was trying to escape my ribs.

He tried to look in my eyes in the dark, his brows knit for a heartbeat, and he made a smile made only for him to know about.

Oh, I know where I am, Miss Sarah, he said. But sometimes I have to wonder about you Tennessee folk, what you're doing here.

This kind of talk always made me sad, for its various reasons, but tonight the sadness I felt felt like it was mine and not the world's. He wanted me to hit him, I guess was how that worked out; it didn't make me feel any better, though, because my heart had hoped for the other.

What this is, sir, is Dawson land and don't bring up that nonsense when you're standing on it, I said.

You're a funny one, you are, he said. Gumption you got for certain.

What I got, I said, is no patience for silly boys out skulking around in the middle of the night, playing raiders or some such games.

Ain't playing no games, he said. Ain't no boy neither.

We will talk about what we are talking about until we are done with it and we are talking about your sneaking around our place in the middle of the night. Now what are you doing here, I asked. Stealing chickens?

Instead of answering he raised his right hand and ran it over his face. He seemed to slump some, sink into the earth a few inches like a post you'd sunk for fencing.

You don't have much of an opinion of me, it seems, he said.

Oh, I have plenty of opinions of you, I said. They're just not the kind of thing you'd talk about in church or amongst polite company.

I was maybe a little too pleased with myself, but he was making it too easy for me.

Simon said you was plucky, he said. You'd have to be deaf to not know he was making fun, that lilt in his voice.

If plucky means smart, then I guess that boy is right about something, for a change, I said.

He laughed, he actually laughed, and raised his arms some, flapped them like he was some bird shaking the dust off.

My, I think I am enjoying your company this evening, he said. We'll have to do this again some time, don't you think?

I felt heat rise up through me and burn my face and I was glad the dark hid it from him. It confused me because my blush had sent all my feelings of anger scurrying into other recesses, leaving only the heat and an immediate awareness of him standing there, tall and shadowed and mocking me. The words that usually stood ready in my mind, dancing from foot to foot, all excited to get out, were suddenly gone shy, hiding in places I couldn't call on, forcing me silent.

Sarah, he said. I got a sister called Sarah. It's my favorite name. She's my second sister called Sarah. First one died, lived two years. Other one's nine.

I've got three brothers and a sister that all died, I said. None a them lived more than three years. All that happened back in Tennessee before we came out here.

My papa done lost ten children over the years, he said. Oldest was Charles, he got to be almost eight years old. Some died so soon they didn't even get names.

They weren't baptized, I said.

I guess that was it, he said.

The night noises played a while, with the two of us standing there outlined from the moon overhead, like lost angels puzzled by a turn of events.

I will see you around, Miss Sarah, he said, and he turned and walked in the direction of his farm. It was a night made nice speaking with you.

His form darkened and lost shape until he was a smudge that itself was soon absorbed by the night.

My eyes rose to the light-filled sky, and I followed the paths of falling stars, if there had been any to see outside of my imagination. I shut my eyes and plotted their arcs, dissecting the sky with graceful slices of light, and wondered if I could will one to spell out my name, the name of a dead girl.

I didn't mention the Brown boy's visit to Simon or to anyone else. Later, when I would think about it, my memory of the night—the interwoven shadows, the icy blue light from the moon, the uncertainty of words—seemed as fragile as any dream. I even entertained the idea that it had been a dream, a terribly convincing dream, the best of its kind.

1960

Dorthea

I smelled the smoke earlier but I ignored it, thought it was just some peckerwood odor, them boys had dropped some food on the floor or the heater, something like that, and I didn't pay it much mind, but after a little while its message got through to me and I said something.

It didn't take them but a second to figure out we was burning up and then things got all hurried up fast as a cat you throw a rock at.

That boy yanked that wheel over to the side so quick I rattled around tween them like a loose bowling ball, then he stood on the brakes and all this rusty, grinding noise roars up around us and I'm scrunched up against the dash, got my face in the damn radio, we stopping so sudden.

Them boys popped out a that car, doors flopping in the hot wind, me scrambling out—I got no intention getting burned up in no white boy's car—and they danced around the front, poking at the hood, testing it for hotness, little dark smoke puffs bubbling out the seams, and then the mean one made a stab at it, lifted up the hood in a rush and there was a big swooshing noise and these devilish yellow and red flames was licking away around the inside and I was backpedaling about as fast as I could, next thing I was on my butt in a ditch. One a them got some old blankets from the trunk, and they's flapping at that motor, them blankets flying in arcs like big crows trying to get off the ground, slapping that fire silly, the flames slowly going down, then all turned to dark smoke you could now see curling up into the stars that was everywhere.

They whipped those blankets at that thing for another minute or so, until they was no more smoke getting made, and then they edged closer, peeked in, saying things to themselves, shaking they heads, and the one, John David, starts giggling. Not that laughing giggling but more that nervous, I-done-lasted-through-everything giggle. Nothing funny about the sound coming out a him.

The other one, he's leaning against the fender on both arms, his head bent down and I heard him saying something about his daddy gonna kill him for permanent this time. I wanted to laugh some myself but I wasn't never that stupid.

At about the same time, they looked at each other, someone said something and then they both looked around, saw me there in the ditch, still on my butt, my dress, they's noticing, bunched up around me, I hadn't moved a twitch that whole time.

It seemed a lot darker than it had been only a minute before, even under all that starry sky, them twinkling lights like decorations put up there by some rich person.

John David came down to me and stuck out his hand and I grabbed hold and he pulled and there I was standing right next to him, him smelling like he stored all his best shirts in a stinky oil drum you'd used to cook pork. He grinned like he at a loss for what to say, like he couldn't get his words straight. I got myself arranged right, slapping at my dress, knocking off dirt and weeds clinging to me like bugs on a screen door.

We stuck here? I asked.

Don't know, he said. He looked up at the other one, still leaning against the car, asked him if he had a flashlight, and that boy said, look in the glove box. He nodded, went and reached in the car, and came out with a light he turned on about halfway back to the open hood, the beam darting across things, making a slice of night colors that was gone before you could remember them. He leaned over, pointed the light into the hole and you could see right away it was like when you let the fry pan on the stove too long, all caught there in the ghost light.

He leaned down in there, moving that light around, shadows shifting like people dancing in some dark club, him making little noises, straining to see better, the other one shuffling back and forth, trying to get his own look.

I don't know, said John David, looks like it just could a been some oil spilled on the motor. Might be okay, then he looked at the mean one, him nodding like he agreed or maybe just hoped they got it puzzled out.

Let's give it a try, and the one driving went back and got in and sat there, his face puffed up taking a couple deep breaths, then turned the key, and damn if it didn't start right up, sounded just peachy. The other one got a big old grin he beamed my way and I grinned right back because I hadn't quite been able to envision walking all the way back downtown and I knew damn sure no one was gonna pick up no negro girl in the middle of no night.

We crowded back into the front, me saying I won't be trapped in no back seat, some fire breaks out, the driver one thinking that was pretty funny.

The beer was down to a couple cans so I offered to share one. The nice one, John David, he said sure, but the other one said he'd just take one by his self, the last one. Guess sharing beer with a negro wasn't his idea of proper behavior.

We drove for a while before I realized how quiet it was, no one talking and the radio been off since the fire, so I turned it back on and some old blues man was crying his heart out, his fingers making that guitar ring through the car.

1954

Osawatomie was set to celebrate its centennial and encouraged the usual things, old-time clothing and bunting draped from all the downtown buildings. Men were required to have some kind of beard or moustache during celebration week, if not the whole year, and when my Daddy went downtown without any facial hair he was arrested and thrown into a jail run by the Rotary Club. He had to pay a fine to get out. That weekend he started a moustache that grew in gray so he borrowed Mama's mascara and painted it over.

The centennial was highlighted by a huge night-time pageant in which the town's history was enacted on the high school football field, the whole town seated in the stands along the west side. It was one of those chilly early spring nights, the smell of popcorn was in the air, people were excited, talking a lot, calling to each other, slow to be seated on time and then the big game lights dimmed and it was like we were all in an outdoor theater and this field the stage and we watched history acted out.

The show started with the story of how the various Indian tribes moved into the area, the Kansa and the Pottawatomi, followed by the early settlers, and then the founding of the town by a small group of New York antislavery immigrants.

We sat on cold, weathered wood bleachers, bundled in wool blankets, everyone leaning against each other for some additional warmth. Out on the football field under the few lights mounted on tall telephone poles stood a small log cabin. It was built to resemble the Adair cabin just a few hundred yards away in the memorial park.

The PA blared that Border Ruffians often raided the early Kansas settlers, and as soon as his voice had echoed off the concrete stadium, men on horses charged out of the north end zone, firing off six shooters and shouting like wild men. They circled the small cabin, shooting at its windows and doorway. From inside the cabin, rifle barrels poked out of the windows, firing back. After a few moments the raiders tore off back toward the north end of the field and the cabin door opened and out stepped John Brown, recognizable from his long black coat and full beard. The crowd cheered as he shook his rifle at the retreating horsemen.

This was followed by the Battle of Osawatomie, when several hundred Missourians under the leadership of Gen. Reid rode up from Fort Scott and burned the town after first battling Brown and his followers. Again riders on horseback fired off guns and a facade of wood buildings was attacked and then burned to the ground.

I loved the noise and the smoke and fire. But I could not understand why Mama hadn't been invited to say something, her being in direct line from John Brown. I tugged on Mama's sleeve and when she looked at me I asked about it, but she told me to hush and just watch what there was to watch. I read ahead in the mimeographed program, maybe something could still happen, explaining our connection to these beginnings.

I hadn't really noticed what was at the end until we got there, the smoke almost all drifted off, rolling between the goal posts, and then one of the men wearing a full dark beard and tall hat and funny suit spoke into a microphone and talked about the Catholic kid and how he needed our help, asked everyone to toss their change into the baskets set up by the exits, help the Catholic kid pay his doctors.

And there he was. While the man had been talking an ambulance drove up and the Catholic kid was rolled out, on his back, strapped to this bed with wheels, his head propped up, looking from where I was like a doll you were supposed to think was the Catholic kid but was not, could not be, the color was wrong and he was tinier and he had none of the Catholic kid's qualities.

A woman down the row in front said, he the one got beat up at school? And her friend saying that's what she heard, a crying shame.

I wanted to say something, I wanted to point out to her that I had not started the fight, that it was not my fault, and that I was blood to John Brown and that it was my destiny to stand up for colored people, but I felt my face hot and when I looked at Mama next to me she was staring dead ahead, her mouth set in concentration. Out on the field men started to take apart the town.

1856

I remembered a day in April when the air was cool but the sun fooled you into thinking it was warmer, so you were fine walking or sitting out in the sunlight but if the wind stirred or you crossed into shade, a chill slid over you like a hand closing over your eyes, as cool as a sudden dark cave. One of those days when you gave yourself up to spring in spite of knowing spring hadn't quite committed itself yet.

I'd strayed away from the garden I'd said I'd turn over, just had an urge to follow my nose and see the new colors just beginning to show, welcome greens and all those tree flowers and prairie flowers. My boots were muddy from where I'd stepped into the soft earth and the bottom of my dress was wet and stained brown that seemed to fade in gradations, like something dipped in tea water.

The voices of birds filled the air with so much noise it was almost like hearing nothing at all, so much of it was like a new kind of quiet, like it was inside my head.

I was paying no attention to where I was going, just going, following the shadows or the ripples in the grass or the direction the young leaves pointed.

The Brown boy stood alone just away from the shadow of a large pine. I guess I'd been looking at my boots because I think he'd been there a while, hadn't just popped out of nowhere but he might as well have, the way he was suddenly there like God had dropped him from his hand, a single die cast on the earth.

His smile was something you couldn't help but look at and think to yourself there was the proof of religion's promises, right there, all lit up with some kind of interior light and mobile to boot. My thoughts weren't even thoughts, didn't have a single word I knew come to mind, but I still recognized I'd thought something I didn't want to explain to anyone, and then I felt my face heat up and I couldn't keep my eyes from flitting around, as though to meet his gaze was simply an impossible act.

So naturally I looked at him as directly as I could make myself, stopped still thirty feet shy of the pine he stood near.

Good afternoon, Sarah, he said, smiling.

Good afternoon, sir.

You know my name. I ain't no sir.

I said it to be the opposite of itself, I said, my voice surprising me with its sound, and I wondered about that.

You out looking for something, wild roots or bark?

I knew he was having sport, though I did not know why. I was exactly divided between being confused or annoyed.

I am simply enjoying the sun, I said. Walking.

That so?

My division was sorting itself out, falling to the side of clear irritation.

And are you merely taking up a new residence under that pine or have you been sent out to think through your problems? I asked, my voice edged like a jagged rock.

He looked around at the tall pine, acting surprised, like he was seeing it for the first time.

Well, now, here I am, you're right, he said, grinning. I guess I am enjoying the day, too. Especially at the moment.

It was only a grin but I found myself startled by its boldness. My mind's slate blank, I grabbed the first words that came along.

My papa says your papa should be locked up.

He met my eyes and then cut away, something on the nearby horizon worth looking at.

He's against slavery, Sarah. That what you gonna lock him up for, not wanting to own another human being?

Niggers ain't human, not all the way, anyway, I said. Any fool knows that.

The thing on the horizon lost its appeal—his eyes bore into mine.

Tell me, Sarah, you seen a lot of dogs and cats in your life—you seen white cats and gray cats and spotted cats and striped cats and black cats—you ever confused about them all being cats? You think one color cat is better than another—not counting your aim might be to match your cat with the quilt on your bed.

It ain't just color, I said. There's more differences. Their hair and noses, how can you not notice that?

He stared at something of interest on the ground and slowly shook his head side to side.

I wonder how someone as smart as you can allow herself to get filled up with such wrong and ugly opinions. I would also like to know why your single topic of discussion whenever you see me is the local politics? I would rather you talk about you, that would interest me considerable more.

I fought my blush but the heat I felt flood my face deepened with my efforts to prevent it. I was pretty sure he was attempting to confuse me, but it wasn't readily apparent what was his gain, other than I would hate him less, which I suppose is goal enough for the kind of people who gauge their lives through the eyes of others. Still, I didn't have to like it.

He looked like he was trying to add a couple big numbers.

Or is that it, Sarah, he said finally. If I show interest in you you feel you have to deflect it by attacking me or my family or my beliefs or whatever else might be handy you can hang on me.

I bet your daddy is wondering why you aren't clearing some land or something, I said.

He looked off toward where some birds were circling, making these high loops over a small stand of cottonwood and oak.

I guess it's your way or no way. My daddy doesn't much worry about what I do. He has other things he worries about.

Oh, I know all about that, I said.

He paused a moment. He looked directly into me.

I am sure you know something, he said, But I doubt if it has much to do with what is the fact of the matter.

I just stared at him, stunned by his arrogance.

You have your point of view, he said. We have ours.

Ours? Yours? Maybe you can tell me what those might be.

You are from Tennessee, here to vote Kansas a slave state. We are here to see it a free state.

Well, I guess that explains just about everything, I said.

That's about what I expected you to say, he said. Then again, my faith in human beings gives me hope in two areas. One, I don't think your mind speaks your heart, and two, you might have learned a thing or two since you moved here.

I've learned that young men from the north haven't been taught manners.

I was too aware of my skin surfaces, every hair registered a breeze or the flutter of a passing bird's wings, the tingle of sunlight, the spread of color in my face.

All of them? he said.

Only the ones I've met.

My feet wanted to run, seemed stalled only by the barest indecision, gains weighed against losses, and the question of why I cared.

And what would be your advice to these ruffians?

His grin was getting out of control, his self-satisfaction roaring through him. But he wasn't looking at me mean, just maybe too joyful, too knowing, and I didn't know what it was he thought he knew, that could make him so rude and friendly at the same time.

I would tell them to take a vow of silence and work harder in the fields.

Nothing about our negro brothers? he said.

We want to take care of our own.

Taking care of your own is the calling cry for just about every kind of trouble, he said.

And what would you prefer?

He stood quiet and looked at me deep and hard, so hard I swear I could feel the light from his eyes inside me, bouncing around like a small bird caught in a room.

We should take care of each other, Sarah. That's what I believe. It ain't part of the politics of anything, it's just a code to live by. The sad truth, for me, he said, is that what I prefer doesn't much figure into the story.

Let us pretend we are alone in this world. Tell me.

We are alone in this world, Sarah. Each of us. It's just lots and lots of us single beings in a world without pity. We need each other more than we need anything we'd ever get alone.

Most days my dream is to climb the Lookout and find a warm place in the wildflowers and lie there and shut my eyes and sleep my life away, right on through winter, if I could. Just step outside the world and its pain.

He turned in a circle, his hands in his pockets, his eyes now flying over everything, maybe not seeing any of it, just sliding from one part of the landscape to another like water.

He seemed the loneliest boy in the world to me, saying that to someone he hardly knew, coming from the family he did. I knew there were no words in my heart could fix all that sorrowfulness. I knew he needed something but I couldn't pin down what it was, though I sensed it flitting around just out of touch.

That's about the stupidest thing I guess I could say, isn't it, he said when he'd stopped scanning our surroundings. His eyes returned to me and more heat washed over me like I was being dipped in fire.

I opened my mouth to speak even though I hadn't the sliver of an idea what would come out. I felt my lips form a circle but not a single word came out of the bubble of my mouth.

I know some kind of noise came out, I saw his eyes register something before I whirled around and ran away. My feelings had swollen up so big they'd pushed me out of that clearing, pushed me all the way back to the garden where I fell on my knees and yanked weeds so fast my hands blurred.

I don't know if I could say I listened to the Brown boy, but I did find myself considering things I hadn't considered, taking stock of what I took to be facts. The world often surprised me but generally it seemed stretched out before and around me like a large colorful blanket. I knew or thought I knew its wrinkles and folds and unkempt areas, knew its colored patterns and how they connected to each other and to the other things. I flat accepted what my eyes were used to seeing.

I never considered there could be other, additional patterns, or that what I saw actually put together a different pattern from one I'd always seen there before. It made me dizzy, made me feel like falling down and spreading myself out flat, grabbing the earth, hold things in place.

Papa said we had no political views except if the government intruded in our lives then we had the same opinion as any of the rest of them: butt out. From what I gathered from the talk and the broadsides, if you wanted trouble, get yourself up to Lawrence where it seemed trouble grew up out of the ground like stubborn weeds.

The other thing, the thing that always seemed to accompany the Brown boy as much as his preachings on slavery, I couldn't even think on that, it just seemed impossible to pin down. I took to thinking on it when I put myself to bed, those times I wasn't so tired I fell asleep soon as I put my head down. I puzzled my feelings. I knew what going all weak-kneed and heating up and losing control of your tongue generally pointed toward. I had read it but better than that, it just didn't need much interpretation. It spoke a language that defied coding, its truth as obvious as air. But how could I harbor such feelings, permit such feelings, for someone I despised, who only enflamed my fighting spirit.

I could not make it unbalance, they canceled each other and so I took to behaving as though neither was true. None of it was real and so I decided a hundred times a day to ignore him when I saw him next.

1954

The day I fell through the ice the second time was cold with a low gray sky so smooth it looked like dirty ice so that when I stepped onto the frozen pond I felt like I was caught in a movie dream, the scenery painted the same dull color.

As usual I skated by myself, darting and gliding from one end of the oblong pond to the other, practicing my new fancy ice hockey stop, something I'd seen on TV. If I did it right, a rooster tail of ice shavings flew forward like diamonds sown to the wind.

There were just three or four of us on the ice. Me, Martha, Woody, maybe Dina. You never knew when Dina was around half the time, the way she was so quiet.

We didn't play any games, just skated the ice, cutting across each other's trajectory, that sizzling sound as loud as our voices, which mostly carried yips and whoas and watch this over the frozen pond.

We fell a lot, sliding in lazy spins until we stopped, laughing, our gloved hands searching for a grip, pulling our knees under us to make our way back to our feet, start all over again.

There was nothing about the ice that was like anything else we did. We didn't turn it into a war game. We didn't chatter much. It held us in a kind of solitude between its twinned silver-gray sides, like we were caught between pieces of thin glass under a microscope, Kids, Spinning.

Someone was over on the far side, off in the trees a little, almost like he was hiding, watching. I skated that way, but couldn't get close because that was the end, if the ice was thin, that was where it would be thin. Every year it was that way, everyone knew better.

From here on it gets dreamy. I know I knew better, but as I skated closer, could see it was a boy and I thought it looked like the Catholic kid. I could see a pea coat and one of those Navy watch caps, pulled down over his ears and right on top of his eyes, coat collar up, just a little bit of pink skin peeking through, like a redhead's. Watching. Hands stuck in the coat pockets. Not moving.

It couldn't be, I said to myself, but every time I glanced over, it looked more and more like the Catholic kid. I skated back toward the others, made a big curve, floated back toward the kid, every kind of question going through my head—how could this be, I asked. Has he recovered, is he well, has he come to watch us skate?

He made me nervous, standing back in the trees. I thought about the fires. The dead colored baby. The fight.

My thoughts went crazy. Everything went through my head. Everything.

I knew it wasn't him, knew with a kind of certainty that seemed unquestionable, I didn't know where it came from, I just believed, insisted, it could not be him.

I was a little scared.

Which was probably why I wasn't paying so good attention to what I was doing. In spite of all that was going on in my head, in spite of my half-believing the shadowy figure back in the trees watching us, watching me, was the Catholic kid, I was showing off, a little leap, pivot midair, come to a slushy stop, spread my arms wide, Here I am, take a bow. Top this.

So I thought I'd do it for the Catholic kid or whoever this was, show him my stuff.

I set out down the ice, thought I cut a fine figure, arms swinging, legs slicing back and forth, body bent forward, going for the goal. Looked up, just to make sure he was there, straightened, did my jump, my pivot, came down, the edges of my skates about to bite into the ice, expecting that nice sound, that spray of ice slivers.

But what I got was a sound that didn't register at first, and then that other sound, a loud crack, and the loud burning pain of incredible cold as I plunged through the ice.

It took about the time it took to think it. I was under the ice, more awake than I ever thought anyone could be.

1856

I flew more often, floated over the yellow grasses, soared over plump cottonwoods and black oak and jack pine—marveled at the orange-spotted rock exposed on flat hilltops, fallen timber, some of it there long enough to be gray and chewed up—today, wheeled and sliced down in a long dive, my eye on something like a movement caught in the tree line east of our land, flashes of color, muted red or a brown, the shiny flushed pink of wet skin, or perhaps the dulled glint of steel off a knife or a bayonet or a pistol.

Later it rained. Horses edged into a clearing, their riders wearing raincoats, hats pulled low, brims pointed down, rainwater pouring away. Three of them, in no hurry, letting the horses pick their way carefully across the muddy ground. The Browns were to the right, our place to the left, the three horsemen moved exactly between, and away, northward, toward Lecompton or Lawrence.

There was hardly any noise, just the clop and suck of hooves and the splatter of water on once-dry leaves and broad puddles.

The riders never raised their heads, just a steady bobbing along under the nattering of the rain on their hats and slickers.

They seemed none of my business.

I allowed the wind to take me toward the Browns, rose over the dark hill, swooped down their side. A light shined through cracks in the door and the shuttered west window, an oil lamp's dull yellow, turned low. Shadows, moving.

In front, too many horses, all stood heads down, rainwater ran the length of their long necks and puddled under their legs.

Voices, almost loud enough to hear, rose through the chimney, mingled with the warm smoke, words and smoke washed away by falling rainwater, its whoosh nearly drowned out flapping wings, boots heavy on boards, angry cries, shouting, a building thump thump thump of feet stamped in unison and then crashing to stop with a final stomp and the cry, Avengers!

Soon they poured out, scattered to their horses, heads down, mounted, nodded at Old Brown and sons gathered on the porch, faces grim but uplifted in purpose, goodnights said, horses kicked, the trail of them, five men hunched over their horses, splitting at the road, two north, three south, then one by one they broke off and returned to their homes, alone and wet, and over them, a bird too dumb to stay landed in such weather.

1954

I see it all from overhead, as though I am suspended from a crane, or can fly, like in dreams. I watch the kid stiffen, then wheel and run into the surrounding woods, and then I am in the water, under the ice, I am sure of it because my head is banging against something and I can tell there is only water, no air, I am under the water, I feel it everywhere, and I am starting to wonder about my next breath, if I get one, when everything swirls and I begin to rise, breaking surface, something heavy draining away, then pulled, dragged out of the water, along the ice, a slow headfirst slide into home, gasping for breath, thinking about the dam of sludge I am building up beneath me, how incredibly cold it is, how soft and wet it is, then noticing my left arm stretched out, being yanked along, hooked up there to someone, a dark shadow pulling me. I hear someone's breathing, heavier than mine. We are jerking along, getting there, and then we are there, the frozen earth, rocky, slick, panting, pumping out steamy clouds of noise.

I roll to my side, look up. It is the Catholic kid pulled me out, his face as clear as a picture.

Afterwards I learned that when the kid ran into the woods he went to find a stick he could use to break up the ice out where I was after he'd slithered out on his stomach, used the fallen branch to smack open some holes, me popping out of the second one he made, then just pulling me out, dragging me to the bank where some neighbors came to us and took us to the city hospital.

Later, in the same room. Activity slows, noises subside to individual sounds: footsteps, a voice in the hall, something pumping, an insistent beeping; an occasional nurse or attendant peeks in, gives a ten-cent smile, disappears. The two of us lying there, piles of blankets tucked in all around.

I am vibrating. Not even a full quiver, just a steady, almost sub-sonic vibration as I shiver under the blankets.

One of us looks at the other; eventually the other looks. Our eyes meet, and there, no more than four feet apart, clearly, I swear, the Catholic kid, and on his face, mottled red and pale, the same question that must have shown on mine. I looked away, no words came out of my mouth though a bunch or two fought for position, all jumbled, uncertain how to sound.

Why'd you do that, I asked, not looking at him.

What'd you say, he said, the voice low, odd sounding.

I slept, I awoke, sucked on crushed ice my Mama fed me with a spoon, and slept some more.

Then I was awake, my Mama was gone, and someone was hovering by the other bed, a big woman.

You got your life saved, the big woman said to me. My boy done pulled you out that pond, least you should do, boy, is know who done that. We don't know who you been talking to but we are Baptist.

I met her eyes and she held me there like I was pinned to a board, and then I chanced a look at the boy and saw right away I didn't know him, some older kid, not the Catholic kid at all.

Thank you, I said.

Afterwards, when I was back in school, it was never talked about. No one knew what to say so generally it was ignored. It was forgotten that I had said, over and over, the Catholic kid saved me, the Catholic kid saved me.

After a while I claimed I'd never said such a thing. I'd hit my head, after all, I said to them. And then I'd screw up my face, let my tongue hang out, and make an idiot noise.

1856

The Brown boy loped down the road and then up our way, fast-walked to where Simon was working with Papa and after nodding to Papa, grabbed Simon and took him aside where he whispered and gestured and seemed generally agitated.

You watch him at all, you see that boy was permanently agitated, always shifting himself around, leaning on things as though his legs couldn't do the job alone, pointing at things that didn't matter to anything. He was an overall nuisance of wasted actions and breathy exclamations. He'd get excited watching corn dry on the stalk, thinking maybe if he watched long enough he'd see some popcorn, I swear.

Simon looked around while he listened, his eyes bouncing off things like scattering marbles but every now and then making sure to take a peek toward Papa who hadn't broken his routine, the two of them supposed to be repositioning some bales from the shelf over the stock shelter but Simon now over conspiring with the Brown boy.

I got to work, Oliver, said Simon.

Just think about what I told you. This ain't gonna happen everyday, Simon. It's what we talked about.

Yeah, I know. His eyes slowed, rested a little longer on each thing he saw. I smiled when it was my turn but he hardly noticed, my attention long ago made invisible by its sheer omnipresence. I was behind the Brown boy so maybe I was invisible to him too though he must have registered me when he come rushing up. He had looked focused, I decided.

Simon followed the movement of a bale from the bottom of one side in a smooth arc up onto the stack on the other side, catching Papa glance back toward where he stood with the Brown boy.

I got to go.

He trotted back to Papa and bent to him and said something I didn't hear but didn't need to hear. Soon a steady rasp-whish-thump carried across the yard as the two grabbed a bale, exhaled loudly, swung the fifty pound bale up and let it drop with a solid thump.

The Brown boy watched for about the time it took to believe he was interested and then he hurried back the way he'd come, though he did occasionally look back. In perfect truth I don't think he expected to see Simon trying to catch up with him; no, it was more like he couldn't quite put together why Simon would stay and do what he was doing given the option of doing whatever it was the boy had dangled out there.

Simon said he had something to tell me and he grabbed my hand and we went running down away from the house, toward the creek, behind scrub bushes and then taller grasses and reeds, dropping lower closer to the water, the air cooler and fresher, hardly any sky peeking through the cover of leaves, and then even over the thumping of my racing heart and our feet clumping through the undergrowth, I heard the ripple of the water along the bank.

Simon slowed and we stopped just a few feet from the water, moving along fast enough to make tumbling white shapes and a constant low din, both of us resting on our arms braced against our legs, catching our breath and giggling, self-tickled by the dash and Simon's excitement about something.

Our amusement wore off and we sat down on facing logs we'd found and placed there on earlier visits to our secret talking place.

Papa took me for a walk this morning, he said. He looked at me wide-eyed, his cheeks filled from the run, his mouth fighting a smile, like he'd been told he wasn't supposed to but it was bursting out of him.

He told me about men and women, he almost whispered.

My hand flew to my mouth, a noise like a cry or a laugh or fright erupted, my eyes watered, I looked away, I didn't know where to look.

Did Mama talk to you, he asked, leaning toward me, trying to see past my hand, my turned head.

I remembered Mama talking to me one morning a few years before after all the rest had finished breakfast and returned to the fields, explaining my bleeding and what it meant and how we saved what we did, what we were made for for marriage and if we were truly blessed, for love, Mama blushing and even at one point crying, telling me how she truly did love Papa and had from the moment she first saw him when she was twelve years old and the last unmarried daughter.

I nodded my head, still unsure I wouldn't break into a fit.

And you didn't tell me? His voice trailed up into the higher registers.

Simon, I didn't think you didn't know, I said. I thought everyone knew, it's just something that happens in life, is what I believe. If you paid half the attention to our farm you paid to your war talk you'd know more about things that matter.

He started to ask me something, would put together two or even three words but then whatever it was he was attempting to say would fall apart, his words tumble into mere sounds that said nothing and then his voice would trail off and he'd say nothing for a moment and then he'd start up again, repeat the same process, finish sputtering nonsense.

I reached out and gently placed my fingertips on his lips, to hush him, to still his efforts, which were only serving to overheat his humors.

He shook his head, held up his hands, stilling me though I'd said nothing, had nothing to say.

Have you, was all he said.

I forced myself to match his gaze, to not turn away like I had before, he seemed in such pain though over what I had no idea, every part of this talk catching me off-balance, the background seemed tilted, the whooshing of the creek sounding like what time must sound like if you speeded it up, if you could stand in one place and the world was sliding by you at an alarming rate, fast and huge as a train.

All I could do was to shake my head, very slowly, still holding his eyes.

You wanted to? he asked, working up to longer questions.

Brilliant sun-bright red and yellow and green scarves flashed inside my head, filled my vision, my gypsy prince. Every night I sought out special stars and asked about him, if he and his family were safe, what they were doing, or what had been done.

I wondered who Simon would think about, who had he seen that had captured his eye, visited his dreams.

I don't know, I said, finally. It was as true as I was willing to be right then. I had tried to keep my thoughts about the gypsy pointed in a certain direction. I did not encourage nor dwell on what some feelings generated in me, what desires I tried to chase off as they left me stirred and unable to concentrate and filled with something Mama would've called the vapors. Too much body heat must not be healthy, I was certain, we certainly could not survive living at those temperatures for long, so I did as Mama offered, I pictured myself burning from some kind of fever, pictured myself stepping into a cool hillside creek, pictured the surging white water washing away the burn.

You don't know? That means you don't wanna say. Because I don't know how you can't know that kinda thing, I truly do not.

Simon, I said, my face warm which only served to anger me, the treachery of my own body. I am not sure you need to know everything about me; I certainly do not know all there is about you, and I don't believe I should.

Then why you follow me around so much?

Someone has to keep an eye open for you. I don't want anything to happen to you, our brother. I gave him my best smile, it just showed up there on my face, warm and loose.

I watch you too, he said, calmly, one of the voices he used when he shared a secret with me, grave and tiny like years had slid off him and he was less a grown man and still a boy, that voice.

You do, I asked. What do you see? Something else I'd heard in his voice cautioned me, sped up my heart.

When you thought no one was around, he said. No one, he whispered, leaning in, whispering again, no one Sarah. I saw. I saw what you did in your bed.

The bright creek and the washed-out sky and the canopy of glowing leaves gave way in a blink to a thick black curtain that roared like I was inside one of them spring storms, everything twisted and dark.

I burst with shame, with a rawness so real my eyes darted to my bare arms to see if my skin was still there, the jolt of seeing my familiar pink-white skin, I wondered how fast I would drown if I threw myself into the creek, I wondered if I could smash myself hard enough with a rock to kill me, I wondered if I could say something bad enough to Simon that he would murder me in rage. I flew through every word I knew, searching for the ones that would get me what I wanted.

I didn't know those words, I just knew the things they would've described if they'd been, if I could've found them or thought them up or seen them spelled out in a dream.

There was only the one secret, so deep down I hadn't even known it was a secret, so buried I never suspected I would have to look at it or think about or give it a name. I had dreamed myself into a place that was part real and part imagined, it was someone else's arm, someone else's hand, someone else's fingers. Until Simon said he'd seen me I could've believed it had happened in my mind in my sleep, those limbs had not moved, had not pushed aside my dress, pulled aside my leggings, found my nakedness, found waves of feelings I didn't know could be felt, afterward lying on my side, curled up, sobbing from the release of something. I didn't know what it was, nor that it had even been there before, but at that moment I was beyond explanations, the only thing that mattered was the sensation of sensation, the total awareness of every part of me and knowing it was fleeting and important and perfect, even as it faded, became a memory that lacked definition, became a single word I could not pronounce, could only be recalled by touch.

I seen you, he whispered again.

I felt a flame consume me, one second it was not there and the next heat poured off me like a blacksmith's furnace. My eyes locked his in a snap of a finger, he recoiled, his eyes big.

I do not believe you have any inkling what you think you saw, our brother, I said. I believe you have allowed Papa's talk to muddy your brain. I believe you are a silly boy and I am disappointed in you.

He said nothing, not right away, but looked at me, shadows passing behind his eyes, his face showing all the things he wrestled with, picking the right words; then his eyes narrowing, his mouth turning down.

I seen you, sister Sarah. I seen you and I may not know what you was doing exactly, I believe I grasp its intention. I believe I know what I saw, in the general sense.

And he smiled, his Simon smile, the one I had no chance against, one that took his whole body and set it at ease and expressive of joy and love and true self.

Yes, I said, I guess you did, you saw me, our brother.

What was you doing?

Maybe you didn't see all you said you seen.

I seen enough, he said. I know something was going on, you was hiding something.

Yes, I was.

He watched me. I felt my heat settle, I felt the creek bank under my legs, I felt the air on my face.

What?

I was touching myself, Simon, I said, almost a whisper.

Why?

I cannot tell you, Simon, I said. I could show you, I thought, and the thought rushed through me like a lightning bolt, a fire roared inside my chest, my face burned all over again.

I said it aloud or thought that I said it aloud. I saw my hand reach for his, and then I saw my hand clasp his and pull it slowly toward me, toward my lap, my smile as strange feeling as my fingers holding his. In my mind, I stood atop a rock cliff and my foot had lifted on its own and a first step into air had been taken. My body teetered and twisted and then tipped and fell, spinning like a dry leaf, tumbling into a pit that rushed up to me but yet had no bottom and was, in the end, filled with too much light.

My hand became his hand and then his hand became more and then there was nothing left but what we did, our hands and ourselves entwined like snakes in a whirlpool.

Later, I awoke and Simon was off and I hadn't seen him leave and I wanted to scream but there was no point. I felt like I'd left the earth and become a creature that lived on the moon, something that was shaped like a human girl but was in fact sculpted from white dust and had a secret life where all that was real on earth was backwards on the moon, where creatures sought something that resisted naming and where sensation was the new air.

I dressed myself and worried away from the creek and up to our place where I walked around like I was still asleep and looked for Simon but he wasn't anywhere. With every step my mind poured acid into my ear, thoughts burning away all the good I once believed about myself. What had I done? What had we done? Is this what happens when you trust your words past the point where they make sense? Did my talk about sin and nature drop me on a trail that I should have known would lead to the place I now was? There were so many words bunched together in my head, so many pictures I tried to brush away with even more words, I knew to the bottom of my feet that I'd crossed into territory where even the rocks and dirt on the ground posed questions.

I asked Mama if she'd seen him leave or did he say where he was off to, and she said, No, I guess not, looking toward a window, and then her attention and hands flew back to her work.

A cold ache spread outward from my heart, and any thought of Simon set me trembling. I screamed his name inside my head, the noise something between a cry and a shout, and only I could hear the last lie I told myself when I allowed his name to re-enter my heart. I did not know if I could bear myself.

* * *

When the family joined for supper that evening, Simon would not meet my eyes though his face and neck looked ripe as a late summer tomato. I said nothing and went through my duties and said nothing some more and after a while enough work done I turned in and stared at the blackness inside my head when I shut my eyes. If a picture even tried to show itself, I shooed it away before it'd settled into focus, didn't matter what it was, it wasn't allowed, all I wanted that night was more night.

It went like that enough days until I didn't have to think about it, it was just what I did, I managed.

1960

John David

The night seemed a lot smaller after the fire, like its heat or
burst of light had burned off a layer of something and things
were now pressing closer. I was holding a beer me and Dorthea were
drinking, maybe half gone. Woody'd gone through the other one and
he sent it over the roof with a flick and I turned my head and watched
it skitter off into the ditch, reflecting just a snatch of light from the
stars like a dime seen from just the right angle on a sidewalk.

That boy can play, said Dorthea, and I said, What? Not knowing
what she meant.

The radio, she said.

I didn't think I'd heard it until she said something, the guitar
notes now somehow jumping out of nowhere, these screaming sounds,
someone's pain with a drum beat holding it up.

You like the blues, she asked, handing the can back to me, just a
little sloshing around in there.

I don't know a thing about the blues, I said. I barely knew what
to call it, the music we were listening to.

It's the truest music of the heart, she said, serious, her head
bobbing.

Nigger music, said Woody, looking our way, then back to the
road where the headlights seemed to pull us along like the long white
string of a pull toy.

The man on the radio sang about how terrible it was to wake up
alone after waking up next to his girl all that time, the guitar leaking
notes in time to his sad heart. It was the only noise we had to hide
behind after what Woody said.

I felt something break loose inside, as though my friend's words had scoured away the paste I'd used to bind things together. I felt afloat, like I could easily lift off the seat and drift out the window, spin off into the sky, be the first man to get to the moon, and I didn't know from what.

There is some of us, mister, she said, who do not care to hear that word.

I don't know why, but I liked her a lot for saying that, like it needed saying and my knowing it hadn't been enough until I heard it aloud.

Do I care what a nigger thinks about what I say?

Woody, I said, then going silent, no other words there to follow on the heels of his name.

Yeah? he said. What? You gonna stand up for this nigger girl? You gonna take her side against me?

His voice had barbs that ripped away more of me.

Woody, come on, you don't have to say that.

The girl stared dead ahead, like she was seeing something out there just in front of the headlights, knowing, I knew, what we saw right before we saw it.

Something caught my eye, and Olathe jiggled in the side mirror, a collection of spilled lights left out overnight. I found myself thinking about what had changed over the last few hours, how I'd talk about this.

Oh, no, said the girl, squirming, pushing back like she could shove herself into the back if only she could get traction. That fire's back, she said, sniffing hard, her head now whipping from me to Woody.

I looked at her and then at Woody, sniffed some myself, and I believed she was right.

Pull over, Woody, now, I said, but before my words were out of my mouth the car seemed to fill with dark, oily smoke and Woody was saying things and stomping on the brake, getting the car off the road, all in about the time it took to talk about it.

Both doors flew open before the car came to rest, me and the girl tumbling out, entangled, bumping and skidding across gravel and dirt and road trash, knocking each other about, my eyes open, registering whirling clouds of dust caught in the headlights like angry ghosts trapped in the daylight.

There seemed to be a storm of some kind, howling, the car at its center, and an orange glow reaching out for something else to coat with its strange brilliance.

I wobbled to my feet, saw the girl off to my side on her hands and knees, crawling slowly down deeper into the ditch, her legs and hands chugging along, her head hanging down and some kind of low noise coming from there. She looked back, saw me, her mouth moving, and that noise still there, hanging in the air like a bubble that could burst into something worse than nothing, but I couldn't really hear her over the crackling and popping and a roaring, like a plane, and she just crawled off into the dark, out of the pool of light given off by the flames fingering out from all around the car, where then I saw Woody flailing at the closed hood with a blanket, dancing up and back, slapping at the hood, whap whap whap, not doing a bit of good but doing something, I guess he was thinking, and then I heard him, yelling at the car, or the fire, or somebody, yelling about how damn useless it all was, how all he really wanted was to see some girls, white girls, he was yelling, over and over, as though if he convinced the burning car, it would suck its flames back inside itself, cool its hot metal, repair its peeled paint, make its innards whole again, and deliver him into the arms of something untouched and unquestioning.

1955

Late spring, the air warm and scented with flowers, almost every breeze carried clouds of white or pink petals, the sidewalks and yards sprinkled like fancy sundaes.

Jaimie had returned to school, been showing up every day or almost every day. The weather was warm enough and the schoolyard dry enough that the morning tag games resumed and once again we reigned.

But something was still not right. His eyes failed to sparkle the way they'd once done and he seemed to droop some when he wasn't running, just ambled along, eyes often downcast, his hands shoved in his pockets.

I tried every joke I knew, and sometimes drew a laugh but even that wasn't the same, sounded raspy and made up or like he was practicing laughing, until someday he could do it for real again.

I screwed up my courage and asked him, is your daddy all right, he out of jail?

Jaimie looked at me from the corners of his eyes, then cut away.

He's okay, he said.

I didn't say anything, kinda tipped my head, my eyebrows asking, yes?

He was quiet, like he was trying to get things right in his head before he said them.

He's in Kansas City, I think. I don't know exactly, he said. He shrugged.

He get a job up there or something? I couldn't shut up, couldn't stop myself from wanting to know more.

Look, John David, it's been months since I seen him. He got outta jail and my mama wouldn't let him back, then he was gone.

I leaned forward, lowered my voice. Jaimie, someone told me he beat up your mama and some man. That true?

You a damn fool, John David? You hear too much stuff you think is true just cause someone said it to you. Sometimes people do things they ain't supposed to do, some things can't be left alone, he said.

His eyes were red and he'd never looked at me like that before, like I was one of them kids said things about him behind his back.

I didn't mean nothing, I said. I'm sorry.

You think cause you almost killed the Catholic kid 'bout me you got some right to say things to me but you don't. You ain't got no right to say nothing about me to anyone, anyone at all. You done what you done all on your own, I ain't got nothing to do with it, and you ain't got nothing to do with me, you understand?

I nodded, said okay okay okay, but in my head everything was all jumbled up, I couldn't make the pieces fit back together, and I knew something had changed, been broken like a plate I'd dropped in the sink by accident, and there was nothing that could be done, no wishing, no wanting, no nothing was going to fix it.

1856

I drifted into a field of tall golden grass and collapsed, flung out my arms like wings and in a snap I glided over the prairie, sliding between the cottonwoods and the blackjack oaks, seeing a dot develop into the figure of a boy hop-skipping down the road two-thirds the way to the Adairs. Throwing a rock into a blackberry thicket, the tight web of thorned purple branches quivering like a beat dog.

Banking, I soared overhead, safely out of his rock range, watching his steps kick up red clouds that broke apart as fast as splashing water, and there, ahead and around the turn down Brown's lane, shortening the distance came the Brown boy, his own dust fading behind him a footfall's beat, then dissolving into wisps and then dull yellow veils and then gone.

Oliver was there first and waited for Simon, then at the end, walking toward him and then spinning and skipping along side, both sporting grins as silly as carnival masks. Their laughter took it all out of them after a short bit and they halted their noisy dance and bent over and laughed until the air was clear around them, just the hint of red coating their pants.

There was talk, the weightless sound of the two agreeing on what they'd already agreed on, and then they started down the road away from home, angled east. Trotting like colts, filled with the dreadful excitement of their grand entertainment.

From up as high as the Lookout you could trace back the long, broad reddish-brown signature of a group of men on horseback coming from Missouri, moving at a confident pace.

The two boys picked up their speed and then ran full steam up the road to a grove of large live oaks and blackjacks and walnuts, the road making a long dappled cavern under overlapping branches as thick as a big man's waist. They were instantly high into the trees like African monkeys, each stretched out on his own branch, and from down below if they were seen at all they must have looked like terrible lumpy scars from some disease.

The boys were so intent on the advancing horsemen they never thought to look back and never gave a hint they knew I was there, up my own tree, a little higher, a little closer to the trunk, watching the watchers.

I do not know what I was thinking. It wasn't words put me up that tree, no voice handing out advice. I tingled with something that knew its answer was in the tree.

It only took the first gruff noises to remind me I had some practice with this kind of thing. Unlike the first time, I was mostly unafraid, knowing I had a way out. But I was fearful for Simon and even the Brown boy who did not enjoy any special protection, and them just old enough to be judged worthy of trouble; these men didn't recognize any court within fifty miles, and who knew what kind of prize came to mind if the boys got caught.

I called out, arced up into the sky, called again and keeled over, slid down a wall of air and called again, saw then the trees empty of dark birds, saw them join me, at first in twos and threes but then a cloud of braying crows massive enough to blot out the sun covered the sky and the riders pulled up their horses and shaded their eyes and watched, this thick black mass, roaring and twisting and then you could hear their voices, what the hell? Twister! It's a goddamn twister!

And that was what we were, a black cloud they knew could carry them and their horses back to Missouri, and they reeled around and set back up the road, this time kicking up an abundant amount of dust.

After the air had settled and the birds had settled back into the trees, the noise abating to something almost normal, Simon and the Brown boy scrambled down from their perches and scampered through the grove and then across the field toward our place, their eyes cutting to the far ridge every three or four running steps.

They paid some heed to the sky, scanning for some hint of what they'd seen. I was pretty sure it was something they couldn't talk about or else they'd get labeled funny or worse, hauled away and held down while preachers yelled scripture, then dunked under water, and when it was all over and they were asked if they'd talk about it ever again, they'd shout no, no, no, never again.

I had saved not only our brother but the Brown boy and I could not have said why, other than that he was part of the bargain, there was truly no separating one from the other. Still, there was a powerful thought that even if it would have been possible to save Simon without necessarily saving the Brown boy, I would have anyway, and I could not prevent this thought from rooting in my mind, because the thought that followed was I was saving the Brown boy first after all. When it was going on I had refused to ask the question, just allowing myself to do what needed doing, I would reconstruct the reasons later when time permitted.

William said, These men are serious, Papa. They have come here to fight for something and they could easily see us as the something that needs fighting.

Drury nodded his head and looked at his brothers.

This is our chance to have what we tried to build in Tennessee, William said, and I ain't letting no self-righteous free-state jackass take that from us. Not on my life.

We will not start their fight for them, Papa said. He looked at us all, washed over our faces. But we will discourage them in our own serious way if they start it.

Papa's face crinkled around his eyes.

The boys affected serious expressions and nodded their heads as though their resoluteness alone was sufficient to the cause.

We will do nothing of the kind, said Mama, her voice firm, her eyes bearing into Papa's. Simon's mouth opened, his jaw worked, but William gave him a sharp kick under the table.

We came here for a new start, Mama said. We will not undo that with causes that have nothing to do with us. We will do nothing that will threaten what we are here to do: to start a new life and build a home and keep our family safe.

William and Drury and Simon darted their eyes from Papa to Mama and back, their faces as readable as a school primer.

I do not intend to jeopardize our life, Mahala, Papa said. But neither will we back down if challenged. We will fight for what is ours.

Ours is what is here, this land, Mama said. What is not ours is this fight over slaves and some people's sentiments about them slaves. God did not give us this gift only to have it taken away by man's politics.

Yes, but we live in the world and politics is around us just like we were in the ocean on a small boat, Papa said. We cannot ignore that those politics run our lives as surely as that ocean's waves and currents and winds.

And then he told us that we would be safe because this had nothing to do with us, everyone could see that. We were here to make it work and that meant going on, getting through whatever was happening around us and making the land hold us up.

I remembered leaving Tennessee and not knowing what to feel, but hoping maybe the unhappiness would go away, the arguing stop, the long evenings of no one talking, each of us wrapped up in our anger like blankets against the others' cold looks.

Papa said it was going to be a different world, a whole new place where it would be like starting new but knowing in advance a lot of things about building a living, not doing the mistakes from the first try in Tennessee. Plus there were more of us to help make it work, get off to a stronger start than back when it had just been him and Mama and the occasional help of some good neighbors.

Well, there was more of us, that's for sure, but you could just about count out the neighbors since almost all of them were free-staters and they wouldn't be caught dead giving us anything.

It was no secret that bands of men on horses had surprised young women alone in the fields and circled their horses, kicking up yellow and brown crop dust, tethered by the standing men, as they took their turns violating her, not even bothering to remove their leather chaps, the girls left bleeding from ankles to waist and mouths where sometimes they hit her to make her shut up.

I know Papa had talked to Drury and Simon and instructed them to keep their eyes on me, not to let me work alone or be too far away from their help.

Drury, I think, accepted this new responsibility same's he'd been asked to clear the blackberry bushes off the far corner, just a matter of getting together the right tools and then going and doing it.

What he didn't fully understand immediately was that watching over me wasn't an item you could do just once and then put away the tools. It was pretty much an everyday chore and after a short while he started to resent it, like we were tied together by some long rope, whose own weight pulled us both down.

Simon, however, was of two minds. He initially adopted a warrior's expression, chin out, eyes focused on the horizon seeking any movement, furrowed brow, hoping to be the one who first spotted the ruffians. And then he wanted to direct my days, tell me what was best for my safety.

Where I could not go any more. And where I could.

I wasn't in a good frame of mind for much of that. Most days I wished I was two girls, one that worked the fields without a solitary thought in her head and Simon—or Drury or William—watching over me like a sick calf; and the girl who fought imaginary bats in her head, waving her arms, shooing it all away. I didn't want no one watching me because I couldn't stand watching myself.

Simon acted like he was protecting his charge, but any fool looking could tell he was inventing it as he went along, trying on poses like hats at the general store.

I made it a point of losing him. It was easier to do than to talk about, he fell for every trick I tried. When I'd reappear, hours later, or maybe only a dozen minutes, just enough to wind him up like one of those toys, he'd steam around and puff himself out and honest to God stomp his foot, all the time his cheeks like cherries and his eyes glistening.

You keep your distance, I said to him once after I magically popped back into his life having gone missing almost an hour previous.

You ain't suppose to do that, he said. How can I watch over you when you disappear?

You are the one person I don't need watching over me, I said. That is simply not a good idea. Not no more.

He looked away, his mouth moving, either forming hard words or quivering from some other difficulty, it not mattering as I wasn't done.

I will stay reasonably close to the house and you can do your work somewhere nearby. You give me room to take a deep breath, I'll stay upwind of you for now, we can develop a solution, our brother. It is the best I can offer. It is what I am asking you.

He raised his head, not right away, had to wait a man's length of time, but then raised his eyes to mine, said, all right, we can try that. You just don't go getting fancy on me.

I'll scrub plates and cookware and darn socks and, lordy, Simon, I don't know what all I'll do, that ain't your worry; I'm the smart-mouth that has to come up with things to do that keep me close to Mama and distant from you.

Okay, okay, he said, stalking off, but not without me hearing him mutter, she didn't say nothing, not to me, no, but I seen her eyes.

Later, after supper, I followed Simon out when he was sent for water. Used to be that was one of our routines when we wanted to talk about what had been talked about over supper. We hadn't done it in a while.

All the words I should have said took flight, leaving me with nothing but regular things, my mind guiding my heart's wants into areas better suited to a boy and his sister out fetching water.

I asked him about his friend Brown. Had he thought about that boy's daddy and all his friends? Could be a bunch of Browns come riding over that rise, horses prancing slow and steady like heartbeats. You gonna shoot that boy then, I wanted to know.

His face seemed to ripple with something, then gone, a little too quick to identify.

It will not be the Browns that come after you, he said, his voice higher than normal, higher than he'd wanted to hear, his eyes showing surprise and then, briefly, shame for getting caught pretending.

I cried inside for what I'd lost with Simon, how we were no longer the same, how we could no longer be the same, that was just lost.

Simon burst into the house, an explosion of afternoon light as the door swung open so fast at first I thought it had simply disappeared. A white stripe of sunlight lay across the packed dirt floor and rode up and over Mama and me and Jonah, the three of us in a circle, me and Mama seated and husking corn and talking about next to nothing, and Baby Jonah on the floor poking at a root with a stick.

We all jumped and Baby Jonah squeaked when Simon roared in, corn silk feathered to the floor. Then we giggled, embarrassed by our fright.

Mama, Sarah, Simon said, his voice as sudden and loud as the door banging into the wall.

Mama's face had gone instantly tight, as though squeezed from inside, and her eyes opened as wide as the doorway.

Simon, what is it? she asked, her hands poised over her lap, in one hand a fist of silk, the other locked on a whole ear.

I was furious at him because I knew Mama's first thoughts were of Papa and I could tell from Simon's face, his high color revealing the excitement of outside news and not the calamity of something personal. I wanted to slap him into good sense.

There's a war, he said, his cheeks as blotchy red as early turnips. There's fighting in Lawrence.

Mama's color returned by degrees, and her hands dropped to her lap. For some reason she turned and looked away, at the wall where an extra chair hung and beneath it a large clay pot where we kept seeds.

She turned back to him.

A war? Whatever do you mean?

Free-staters and slave staters, Mama, with cannons and Sharps rifles and generals in uniforms and all, he said, like it was next week's

Saturday market and a special wagon of performers from the east were promised.

Where'd you hear this? I asked, still angry at him for scaring us, for giving Mama whatever thoughts she'd had for that brief moment. That Brown boy?

Simon's expression dissolved into a shade of confusion and then some anger of his own as he understood that his news wasn't received in quite the way he'd imagined, although I am sure he had no idea what his expectations truly were; it was merely that all his forward momentum had run its course and had run aground somewhere short of the shore.

He gathered himself and then said he just learned it from the Brown boy. His daddy is going up there to lead the free-staters. Most the sons going too.

You could tell there was more, like what he had to say next filled the room before he said it. A bubble of words, unbroken.

He set his face and said, I want to go with them.

Mama was still, but her face drained and then filled back with color and her eyes went to ice.

You certainly will not, she said. Your Papa won't allow it. I won't allow it.

She held him with her eyes.

You are too young to know what this is about and you are too young to go to war, regardless.

Simon did his best to glare at Mama but he folded his tent in about the time it'd take to snap your fingers. He studied his boots, then kicked one with the other and dried mud clattered across the hardpack.

This is the end of this topic for you, Mama said.

At night, if the moon was low or new, the Lookout loomed over our place like God, bigger than anything else and weighty with thick blackness, like something about to crash down on us. And you could hear coyotes and dogs and the cries from night birds, owls and some hawks; and something else now, something no one wanted to think about, night lightning or gunfire, and cries that didn't belong to any-thing that flew.

Spring storms crawled across the territory like wild dogs, chewing up the land and people's homes, leaving scattered scraps that the rest of us stared at or rummaged through for signs of something positive, something that had survived the fierce, howling winds. We found bits and pieces, but never anything whole.

The weight of the dark clouds was sometimes too much to bear, and I imagined myself someone from the Bible who had been asked to do more than could be done, just getting through those days, the storms of nature and the storms of mankind.

I just didn't know why people worked so hard to kill each other.

Sarah, the Brown boy said.

That's my name, I said. I don't think there's no reward for knowing that. Then I remembered his dead sister and I regretted my sharp tongue.

He looked down at his feet but then almost immediately jerked his head back up as though he'd caught himself performing and halted himself. Or, I suppose, the other way around was possible too, that he looked down out of true embarrassment and that what came over him was not the withdrawal of a persona but the application of one, he would play The Humble Man.

There was no true clue in his eyes or especially his mouth which rippled into that maddening smile, a smile both as full as a child's and empty like a chalkboard, you write on whatever you want to see, as though he had a knack for looking inside you and knowing what design of smile would make you feel a certain way, guide your heart as surely as though he took your elbow with his hand and gently ush-ered you where he has made you feel you want to go.

I was suddenly aware that my knees were no longer reliable, that the barest misstep, shift in balance would topple me like a broken tree. If I didn't look away or think on something else or develop an armor, I knew I was lost, that this boy man could own everything in me worth owning, there would be no secrets I wouldn't shower him with, entrust him with, and still, sensing all that, a shrill little voice hollered, stop, whoa, nothing of such magnitude can possibly change this rapidly, a person cannot be ripped inside out in an eye blink, all life's knowledge cannot be ignored as though it were suddenly nothing but a fiction.

Yes, but, the louder chorus replied. Look at that smile, dare to look into those eyes, look at the angles and planes of his hands, his long fingers. Let this thing wash over you like you were being reborn, dipped into the river, this river roaring and surging and frothing all around.

I rallied with all my might.

I'm sorry, I said, about my name, about my smart mouth. My head was tilted down just a shade, my eyes raised to look into his. That little voice, what a cat would sound like if it talked, shrieked, what? What words are coming out of your mouth, girl?

Do you think we can truly go back to the beginning, he said. His face flattened, it seemed, into something more serious. We were going to talk philosophy, it seemed.

I do not think I know how to reframe a memory so that it plays differently or is erased altogether, I said.

People forget things all the time, he said. It don't mean nothing.

Certainly I may forget where I left the shears—possibly my mind was occupied by other matters—but I do not accept that I can so easily forget a person's nature or an event that marked me in some significant way.

So you can tell when something happens if it's important at the time, he said. You can know the beginnings of things, the place where something started its journey?

I believe I have a sense of measure, if I am presented with the truthful facts, I said. If I am shown a falsehood, if I am fooled by devious means then perhaps I would not recognize the underlying truth and thus I would not have an accurate picture of events and I would possess a false memory. But remember, for that to happen I would have to have been deceived and so I do not accept that I could be held responsible for what had been done to me.

You accept everything by how it seems, how it looks, he asked.

I must believe in something so I choose to believe that people will tell me the truth if I let them.

And if the truth turns out to be merely another point of view, where does that leave you?

There's some points of view that see everything, from every angle, ain't no place you can hide.

He squinted his eyes like he was having trouble seeing through a glare or maybe he was just thinking extra hard and this is what it looked like. I hoped not.

His squint receded back into one of those smiles, like he was tickling a puppy's tummy. Are we talking about religion now? he asked.

I wanted to slap that smile into the next field. I wasn't a pet he had any right to talk to in such a way, dismiss me like brushing aside a nosy dog.

What we are doing—surely steam flared out of my ears—is not talking about any damn thing, and I spun around as best I could on unsteady knees and set into a march, each time a heel hit the earth it left a hole the size of a goose egg and I seemed to be huffing and puffing just like some actress on a stage and that only made me angrier because I did not, absolutely and definitively did not want him to question for an instant my sincerity, the authenticity of my emotions, and for me to think I sounded like I was giving a performance in much the same way I had questioned his sincerity shook me and then also nudged me even further into my anger only this time I recognized that the true target of my anger was myself, for allowing myself to experience all that I had felt in the last half hour.

Maybe he had no right, I thought, but I also had no right to do that to myself, I had no right running away from the world's veils and masks, from its lies of self-preservation. I had no right to play the fool. I had no right to stare blankly at the writing on the wall. Innocence is nothing more than an acceptance of appearances.

But we were like twined moth and flame, each the one and the other at once. In the most natural ways our paths crossed, more and more frequently, a week between became five days became four and three and two and after two we both had to admit coincidence would no longer pass muster and so we got all shy, frightened and thrilled to have crossed another line. It was like you didn't get to decide, whatever it was you expected to happen didn't happen that way at all and your having crossed over was knowledge after the fact, you'd done it because you were in the vicinity and should have known better.

People are gonna start talking, I said. The morn was clear, and only a handful of plump clouds, scattered like runes, marred the perfect robin's egg blue sweep of sky.

I don't see how, he said.

We were sitting on a fallen log, the old one off the hill path, fat old oak been on its side for a while, worn smooth with weather, bleached near white. My hands were in my lap and he leaned some on his, the one nearest me only inches from my thigh. I was positive I could feel its heat across the space of air and through my dress and petticoats and drawers, feel its press against my leg. I was aware of little else and was sure I had not heard a peep from the woods around us nor from him so intense was my focus on his hand to my left.

If you don't say nothing and I don't say nothing, how's anyone to know, he said. He rocked some, a gentle back and forth, only a few inches travel, and a vibration passed through the log and then into me so that I imagined every fiber of his muscles where they touched the smoke-white log.

I don't have to say a word, I said, but folks know things without them having to be announced. You think your behavior lately has been like it was a few months ago? You don't think your family got eyes in their heads?

I don't think I've gone all silly or anything, if that's what you're getting at, he said. His rocking had slowed, he was nearly stilled, his head turned toward me. His hand between us was tanned and had large veins and looked like it could crush a river stone.

I think I have accumulated many unexplained hours away that I am sure at least one brother has pondered and for all I know one of them has followed me a time or two, to make sure his darling sister weren't in some kind of trouble. One of them could be here now, in some clump of bush hearing everything we say, watching us, waiting.

Waiting, he asked. He couldn't help himself, his eyes searched the area on their own as though he'd suddenly been told there was likely a beast just outside the campfire though it was late morning and we didn't have a fire going.

To catch you doing something you aren't supposed to do. Now his smile was back in place, his back straightened some, his head tilted.

Is there a list of things I am not supposed to get caught doing, or trying? I think it might be a good idea if I knew the boundaries so that a gang of your brothers doesn't bushwhack me.

Oh, I don't think they'd wait that long. I think they'd be more likely to leap out of the countryside and take care of you right here, I said.

I may be faster than they take into account, he said.

Meaning you'll get away.

Meaning I'll do my wrong and also get away. He smiled his full smile and I made my eyes stay on his though it felt like there was a firebox in my chest and each second I looked at him I fanned its flame.

I hadn't seen it or even felt it but I looked down and his hand now covered mine, warm and not as rough as I'd imagined and not still as he gently massaged and touched my hidden hand and then with his encouragement he turned my hand and our palms joined and I trembled like a little bird teetering on the rim of its nest.

If you have something to say to me, Oliver, I think this is the time, the words sounding a raspy whisper from deep inside, still more words unmade and lost in my long exhale.

Sensation for its own sake governed my desires. I was hungry and I ate every scrap and I ate like I had no manners, stuffed food into me, picked wild berries, snuck fruit from neighbors' trees and I got smaller, thinner, not fat. I was consumed with a nervous energy, my whole being focusing on one thing, on the single part of my life that changed everything, on the feel and taste and sound and smell of it all and it was almost more than I could stand, my raw hunger. I shamed myself, if only to myself, but my thoughts brought sudden flushes to my face and Mama would ask if I was well, and I would say, yes, Mama, I'm fine, and maybe I'd have to add something on, say I was winded or had swallowed something the wrong way and all along the memory of the thing sent a smile to my lips I did not want to have to explain.

I was not so stupid as to think there could not be consequences, it was just that we had no idea of their nature. We talked plans, about what made sense, what we wanted. It was soon clear to both of us that we hadn't thought a lick past our first touch. We were still trying to figure it out and we didn't have a goose's sense about what to do except discover all we could about each other.

Our bodies took everything over, the sweaty quiet drumbeat we made became the only tune we heard. And we laughed more than we did anything.

I did not know what we would become. My world was aroil with its complications, all of my own making to be sure. My heart was bursting with too much of everything, my nerves so tingly it almost hurt to wear clothing, everything seemed brighter, louder, sharper, sweeter or more bitter. My senses embraced the world with enthusiasm and I was both exhausted and stimulated by it, wanting to run through a field and retreat to sleep at once.

And at the time I didn't give it notice that what I did or what I had become was in any way a diversion from what I'd done or become when I'd spent that afternoon near the water with Simon. It should have been clear to me that perhaps some of what controlled me was my fear of myself and that what I sought from the Brown boy, all I was doing was seeking refuge from the parts of me that I'd come to believe wanted to smother me.

My heart felt bound up like a madwoman so she wouldn't hurt no one or herself.

1960

Dorthea

I scrabbled away from the light and the flames, knew my dress was getting ruined but I swatted that thought aside and hightailed it down the ditch, the headlights making tunnels of light up left of me, pointing toward some place that weren't burning down, was how I looked at it.

I could still hear that boy whaling on that poor car, and him yelling something I could just about imagine, him being a junior Klan man for sure.

I stood, wobbled some but said to myself it was just the ditch's doing, trash and rocks and even some water trickling down the middle, my eyes dropping to my dress and seeing it now just about the color of the night, smudged and soaked and torn and hardly a dress at all no more.

I could barely raise my eyes but when I did they snapped on that car a ways back, ball of red light trapped under the hood, then the mean one throwing open the hood, and both them boys swinging their coats, and the glow fading so's all I saw was the headlight glare and both boys leaning against the car, one on each side, both staring up at the stars, and then the mean one wiping his head with his sleeve and then turning and then shining a flashlight at the motor, and them talking, but it was just whispers to me.

No more white boys, I said to myself, they is nothing but trouble, it is just God's own truth, and I best pay more attention in this world or the bad things that visit my dreams will stop pretending they is dreams and take on forms.

There was no small part of me that was steamed at Delbert though it ain't his fault I dote on him like I do. If I didn't see his good heart I wouldn't trouble myself, but I am the only one in this world who sees into his heart and knows there is good there, and he needs me to remind him of his true nature.

I pointed myself the way I'd been headed figuring there must be a road up somewhere, and besides I wasn't going back toward that car and them two white boys. Whatever was ahead in the dark was better than what those two presented. I put one foot front of the other, worked my way up the bank to dry, level land, and trudged into the dark.

1856

When I was five, maybe six, back in Tennessee, in the first days of a brutal winter—winds howling like beat dogs, snow driven straight across like thousands and thousands of white horizons or slashes in the dark blue-gray sky—the fever got me, had me in a grip like a man's fist. The world had gone boiling on me, heat rose off me like my head was a stove, all I looked at seemed rimmed with red fire, like a skin of blood coated my eyes. Mama squeezed out wet rags and lay them on my head and I'd dry them with my heat in a matter of minutes. Sounds scalded my ears and seeing objects sent needles into my eyes and just lying there on my tick mattress felt like I was atop a tangle of blackberry thorns. Everything about the world hurt and confounded me. Words tumbled around inside my head and made a sense that only I could understand, in that flash moment but then gone in the next, my views into the secrets of the world like blinks, new and then forgotten with the next blink picture. Nothing lined up right. Things that I seemed to remember making sense now failed to arrange themselves into anything I knew. The color red shaded everything but the word for red was gone from my mind. I saw the red-edged world and the word 'air' was all I could imagine.

I was like that again—except this time it was all inside me, invisible to others but still the world was aflame in my heart.

Only now no one who laid a hand on my forehead would think fever for it would seem cool and was not damp with my heat, no pink rimmed my eyes, yet dreams as vivid as everyday waking filled my vision, words came unbidden to my ears but their meanings slid away like ice away from ice, just noiselessly gone and left behind was a scant trail of light that seemed to want to whisper itself if light could do such a thing, this picture of a word I wanted to hear, to see, to touch, to bring to me and protect with my cupped hands, held like a bird, its heart thudding against my palm, against my breast, then made still with my own warmth. Not a fever's heat but the kind of heat that lets things in this world sleep in its own pocket of love and safety and everything laid out before it like a supper arranged for the kings and queens of the land.

I hadn't thought about the crows for a long time. How I felt them watching me, I think the same ones day after day, sitting and flying away and back, perched atop a dead tree, heads cocked, beak parted, tongues beating like tiny hearts.

I tried not to remember this last time, a time when the view from up high was too much. This was after almost everything, after me and Simon and after me and the Brown boy. I tried not to remember me looking down on the tree tops, swooping over the house, right through chimney smoke, keeling over into a wide turn, away, riding the heat up the west side of the Lookout, shooting over the top and it almost looked like the whole territory was spread out like a rumpled horse blanket, all the way west to a blue-brown bruise that made the horizon, and east to Missouri; overhead, fat white and white-blue clouds piled high like dry sails.

And below Simon and the Brown boy lying amidst a sprawl of waist-high grass, hidden to everything except the crows and hawks circling overhead.

Simon's eyes, wet and bright as twin sapphires, traced the crow's graceful arcs. Deep inside tiny pieces of light registered the bird's noisy cawing as words called out from a page. His bare arm laid across the other boy's bare back, his fingers idly tracing lines only he could see. Their clothes nearby made a tangle that reminded me of gypsy scarves.

A warm air spiral took me up, circling upward, it felt like falling up to heaven. Below, the boys grew smaller, their joined shape a spinning T. Higher yet and they merged to a point and were not boys at all.

The light from the west dropped in a blink from pink to dull red to purple. Black rushed in from the east.

* * *

All the grand things I had said about sin no longer applied. If I had believed it possible for me to ascend to the heavens and from there fire thunderbolts at the Brown boy and at Simon, I would have been out there on the nearest mountain, which almost caused me to giggle as I figured the nearest mountain was the Lookout, as convenient as you could ask for.

I was not a fool, I recognized myself as the kettle, Simon the pot. I guess that made the Brown boy another pot. Or another kettle. I felt like giggling again. I didn't know why I was finding fun when I knew I was supposed to be outraged.

I thought on that a moment. I knew I felt hurt, and I knew that spurred me to hurt them back, them being neither one but merged, then I caught myself thinking that way, joining the two boys together as something I could aim my hurt and my anger at, wondered why I had done that, assumed that what I had seen was the final version, or that what I had seen meant any more than I'd seen. I questioned the pictures I recalled. I shifted the images around, reflected on different angles, peeled my fingers off what I'd believed, let it loose of me, and reconfigured it into something where hardly little was truly known.

My life was bursting with things I did not fully understand and I felt like I was in a traveling show, standing in front of a painted board, facing a crowd of mostly men, and watched as knives flew into the wood around me, outlining my frozen body, knives that were knives but also shimmered with a second manifestation, looked like slaves and angry neighbors and two boys, and I knew that if I moved even a little bit, one of them knives would slice all the way through me.

My mind refused to consider itself any longer. Threw up its hands and walked quietly away. I had nothing to say on the subject, no words were permitted to form and then join into a sentence and then paragraphs crying my sorry story. It was because I saw no solutions, saw no avoidance, saw no combination of words and gestures capable of explaining the progression of my obsessions, the slow almost unnoticeable growth of my hunger and then the still slow unwinding into action, when I submitted to my heart's onslaught, when I no longer believed in the things that distanced me from myself. I gave in to all of me the too-sweet pain of too much, of exposing every fiber of my senses to the things in this world primed to play like a piano my heart.

I gave myself to the pleasure of myself—this world cannot be God made and not balance pain with pleasure. If we are asked to suffer then it follows we are permitted pleasure. It is how we know one from the other, their contrast. One is unable to be without the defining other. The natural world holds itself in balance, I don't think it could be any different with God, so balance it is and with that comes the whole package, everything and its opposite, I guess you could say.

Each of the world's parts is mirrored in some part of itself, the whole made from the collective opposites of every possibility.

Simon sat at the dinner table and played with his spoon and studied it like he was practicing to be a surgeon. Mama and I were draining off some fat from the big kettle of stew heating over the fire. Carrots and potatoes and yellow onions and green onions and some radish root and bones.

Papa was still outside getting the dirt and mud off before coming in. William and Drury were out there too, William helping Papa, and himself getting cleaned, Papa and him and Drury slapping each other, making puffs of dust, the clatter like mice of pieces of dirt fell to hard-dirt porch, loud brushing off and kicking their boots against the steps.

Simon looked even dreamier than usual but these dreams reeled with something he didn't want to name, his eyes trying to find some place to hide.

I didn't feel one way or the other about it.

Not all my own dreams or flight visions or words I hear whispered at the oddest times, not all of them turn true. Some, I am sure, never happened, or at least not in exactly the way I remembered it.

We studied it in school, back in Tennessee. We looked through telescopes at things too far away to see without help and then we talked about it and no one seemed to be looking at the same thing, it was something different for every one of us.

It brought things up too close. We didn't recognize things, startled, perhaps, by the scale of our reflections.

But here, now, as I set out plates, Simon came away from his dream and looked at me, no, studied me.

I felt like I'd gone asleep and awakened on a bright-lit stage in St. Louis, his eyes focused on me like sunlight. Then he shut his eyes and shook his head, erasing something inside his head, and resumed deciding if the tableware was up to his standards.

What is going on with you? asked Simon. You are changed. You make me feel like I am unknown, even to myself. No, that is not right. He looked off at the cottonwoods that lined the creek.

I am not getting this right, he said. You make me talk like a fool.

You are not a fool, Simon. You are the heart of my world, I said.

His eyes were brown and yet seemed to have all the gold worth owning.

You may think I don't know but I know, he said. Something has changed. Something has gone out of me, he said.

What did he think he knew, I puzzled. Lately it seemed there was a host of new things that filled up my insides, take your pick of the litter, but how could he sense such a thing? Did I glow like an ember? Was it my cheeks, constantly warm and sensitive? Then, was he judging or sensing judgment? My head spun.

I could not stop a search of my heart, which had started thumping in my chest, afraid to ask, had I not thought of our brother Simon these days, even more than ever? Then how was it possible he felt ignored?

The recognition turned my insides liquid. I then refused to ask myself another question, I'd had my fill with things I wished I didn't know.

I could not help myself, I looked away. I sought help from the voices that rode the winds, heard myself ask for the things to say: Simon, I said in my head, I am mad with something I cannot name;

I know it is not love or at least not the love I believed awaited me, the kind of love Mama and Papa have. No, this is something raw and selfish. My soul cries for this thing, this sweet pain that I refuse to admit I want or need. Simon, I am lost to something I do not want.

What I said was, Simon, my heart, I am still all I was. It is just the swirl of everything going on around us. You are always with me.

I wouldn't know the swirl that takes you over, sister, as it seems to happen someplace else. Some place, he said, where things are more swirly, I guess.

He looked around, did it like he'd seen it done someplace and the impression had been made, it'd had some kind of winning effect and here he got to try it out, the gesture, the move designed to impart impatience and exasperation and no small part of the world's weight.

But even as theatrical as his behavior was, I felt the tightness of his heart, the hollow balloon of pain under his chest bone. I knew what hurt I caused.

And it was all balled up like yarn by what I'd seen on the Lookout, those two boys and how it made me feel. Each one had some kind of combined grip on my heart, as though one and one added up to three, that in some mystical way I was part of whatever they were a part of and that realization surprised me with how it calmed me, the way seeing a wall of water rush toward you after a spring downpour stilled your fear: the moment for fear had passed, it was already done, this thing that was happening, there was just the eyeblink of light before you'd be sent tumbling downstream.

Simon worried me at all times but no time more than now. Sometimes he looked like he was in a different place, his young man's body shuffling through some chore but his mind off and away. His mouth was slack and dreamy and his eyes reflected no light as they locked onto the texture of the dirt.

I feared where he was because I knew where it was, and I knew exactly why he applied his will to defy nature's laws, why he dreamed he was elsewhere, why he felt a deep nameless tremor that horrified and drew him.

I dreamed it too. But not for Simon's reasons. Mine had nothing to do with proving something to myself, though I suppose you could argue they both had something to do with love.

I imagined it had something to do with the moon.

Like about most folk, I didn't believe myself wicked—I had a notion—no, more than that, a sense of things, a knowledge even—that at the heart of my being I was a child of God, a good person.

But the feelings I had and the thoughts that developed from those feelings were inside-out of what I believed or feared was in my heart, that from my good nature spilled ideas or mere words or desires that gathered unto themselves a blackness that no light could penetrate, no words from a preacher or the Bible could countenance.

Inside I believed that my soul was in a kind of danger—from myself, from my own feelings—that I was willfully piloting a ship into the rocks.

I knew from a lifetime of preachermen that there were words you heard inside you that you wished you hadn't heard or known about, that seemed to betray your best intentions if not your mortal soul but there they were nonetheless, unbidden, banging inside your head, the sounds and meanings as clear as hanging in the spoken air.

The whole question of the hereafter only confused things for me, though, when I thought about it. I didn't fully accept that either salvation or redemption or punishment awaited me at death.

I would lie in bed at night and stare into the dark over my head and try to picture heaven, try to see spread out across the dark an actual place—that had wide paved streets and clean white buildings and groomed horses and glittering carriages we'd all ride in for free.

But when my mind pushed these pictures aside, what was behind them made the pictures themselves false, like something drawn on tissue that then was wet with tears and melted into paste.

I didn't understand how the heaven I pictured could be the heaven of a hundred years ago—did man take to heaven his earthly talents, updating things year by year like here? Did it look now like it did a thousand years ago?

It seemed to me that heaven would be the same always and would in no way reflect our life on earth, yet every preacher talked about reuniting with lost family, like there was a large sprawling picnic on a grassy hillside, all my relations gathered, ready to greet each generation's newest arrivals, give them some chicken or a glass of sweet tea with mint.

What I had exposed in myself deeply troubled me. It was like learning from a doctor that my insides were installed wrong, my stomach was where my heart should be and my heart was where my bowel should be and my bowel was where my stomach should be, through all the powerful organs, that what made me who I was was disjointed or wrong, the way a two-headed calf was wrong. There were ways we were made to be and anything different announces a flaw— or maybe not a flaw but a way of being that was somehow outside the world though its very being joined it with the world, a double bind of being what the thing can be and what the thing cannot be, a spinning plate when the top and the bottom look as one piece.

Sometimes it all felt like we were being squeezed into some kind of funnel, the walls closer and narrower, and up ahead the funnel only getting smaller, the opening so small you could tell that not every part of you would make it through whole.

The night we got squeezed into nothing started with one of those splinter moons that makes folks stop and look up and point and say, look at that, would you, like a slice of onion too thin for anything but scrap, but up there in the dark sky as startling as a razor swiped across the night.

We knew things were going on. All the last two days men and horses and wagons had gone by, some heading west, some back, some, it seemed, lost in circles, the same men and wagons passing back and forth like sentries.

They done burned down Lawrence, Simon said.

Mama looked grim and Papa shook his head, said, They got into it this time.

William said he was now leaning toward joining the Missourians, push the free-staters out once and for all.

Everyone had heard about the posters that had been found all over the Pottawatomie area, all free-staters had until May 25 to leave or be killed. People traveled in groups and more and more guns were seen just about everywhere, even to church on Sundays. It was like being in a storybook.

In my dream we were no longer tired from clearing weeds and rocks and the nests of many small animals. In my dream, Papa did not want to talk about what's going on all around, did not warn us to be careful because we're smack dab in the middle of a battle that just hasn't been named yet. He didn't say, this has nothing to do with us.

In my dream he said nothing. It did not continue. The things that followed did not follow. In my dream we tilled the land, harvested our crops, and tended to our animals and each other. There were no angry men with weapons roaming the countryside, looking for people who disagreed with them.

Papa and William and Drury and Simon were arguing about what to do tomorrow—Papa said we had to clear some land, not lose sight of what was important, and both William and Drury wanted to ride with the Law and Order riders. Simon, off by himself, wanted to know why would we want to die for slavery, it didn't do us no good.

The older boys looked at him hard, turning where they sat.

Boy, I will tie you to a fencepost if that is what it takes. That Brown boy done bamboozled you with fancy talk. You better remember where you're from.

I am from Kansas, Simon said though not very loud.

Outside, the yard dogs raised their voices, and then their barking diminished as they went down the road toward whatever it was got them riled. Then two sharp loud squeals, like something collapsed to nothing in an instant.

I remember looking toward the door as though the answer to the dogs' silence would present itself and explain to us why they'd quieted themselves so. I saw Mama looking too and we met eyes, and that was when we heard the rattle and slap of men on horses and then the door shook from someone knocking too hard.

A deep voice called out Papa's name and demanded he open the door. Papa's and the boys' argument was gone that fast.

Open up, Dawson, we want to talk to you, said the loud voice again. Open the door.

Mama's hands tightened in her lap and she looked at Papa and said, James, that doesn't sound right, do not open that door.

We all were still as things under a hawk's roving eye but then William took a step and reached up to where the rifles sat on brackets. He lifted one down and then reached up for some shells.

Papa said nothing but I could see his face was drawn tight.

What do you want, he called out, looking at the door as though he was talking to a gentleman standing there and not a dull wood door.

We need to talk to you, Dawson, said the voice.

So talk, Papa said through the door. I can hear you just fine.

It was quiet long as it takes to put a different sentence together. This is between men, Dawson. Men talk face to face.

Papa raised his eyebrow at Mama, even tipped his mouth into a hard smile. Mama gave him the same sad smile back.

And gentlemen don't ride up after sundown and bang on people's doors like they was attacking an English castle, Papa said.

William finished loading his rifle. Papa hadn't seemed to notice but when William raised the barrel toward the door, Papa said quietly, lower that right now, son.

I ain't no English gentleman, said the voice. I am a man of God and I act under His guidance.

Drury walked over to where the rifles were and got himself one, started stuffing a shell into it. Simon's eyes flitted from one older brother to the other, pausing over the rifles like they were newly invented implements of some kind.

Papa held out his hand, a gesture that said, hush.

I am sure that God has little to do with what you're here for, said Papa. You are not welcome here tonight and if you think you have rights to tell me otherwise, then you've made another mistake. Now get off our land.

Our eyes were everywhere at once: on Papa, on the door, each other, the rifles. No answers leapt into my vision, just terrible questions that inside I knew would not be ignored.

Muffled voices moved around outside, a clear word here and there, shuffling things, voices lowered, and then something thudding against the door then landing on the porch.

We all jumped when the thing hit and we stared at the door like we could open it with our eyes and safely peek out, see what had happened.

Papa, Simon said, pointing at the door when Drury called out, smoke!

Papa jerked forward and Mama reached out her hand. He touched her hand as gently as you'd stroke a flower and then he stood and strode toward the door. He smiled back at Mama and I could almost hear his voice saying it was okay, but instead he said, we can't let them burn down our home.

Drury and William dropped the rifles, Drury reached for the water bucket and William grabbed the nearest blanket and then they rushed toward the door. Papa raised the bar and the door burst open and five men filled the room, knocking Papa back onto the floor and spilling William too. Drury staggered back into the wall like he'd been hit but he had not.

Outside, another man stomped on the burning sagebrush, then kicked it into the dirt.

What are you doing here, said Mama without hesitation, her voice hard as oak.

It was Old Brown and sons Watson and Owen and Oliver and another man and they were holding sabers, glinting yellow and red light like they were afire. Owen had a revolver tucked into his pants and the stranger dangled a rifle.

This is our home and you are not welcome here with weapons in your hands, Mama said.

Outside, you and you and you and you, said Old Brown, ignoring Mama and pointing at Papa and William and Drury and Simon.

Oliver looked at Simon, his mouth moving but no words being made. Simon's face looked pale and drawn tight, his eyes watery but still somehow flat, like he'd turned a corner and come fact to face with an unknown animal from an unknown country. He looked lost.

No one is leaving our home except you. You have no business here, sir, said Mama, her voice even louder, as though volume was the missing element to their exit.

Woman, said Old Brown, his eyes as wide and dark as ripe black-berries. Your voice goes unheard by me and mine. Stay put.

You are in my house, she said. You will listen to me and I will not ask you again, leave our home.

Her voice had risen more, and Mama's face in spite of her loud anger had grown not red but gray, as though all her blood had drained out and she had become a fierce statue unable to effect action.

Outside, Dawson, said Old Brown, his face a pitiless mask. He stared at Mama and me, words almost visibly galloping across his face. You, pointing at Mama and me, stay or go, it don't matter to me.

Old Brown's sword tip swayed back and forth like a coiled snake. Even his own men couldn't take their eyes off it as it sprayed colored light, its fiery glint counting something I knew watching I never wanted totaled, he could just swing that blade for as long as we could watch and if that is all it came to, that would be my prayers answered, but inside I knew worse was going to be the way this went, his blade too thirsty to be left dry.

In dreams sometimes things move slower than in real life and tonight was like a dream except the words were regular and the people were familiar—I knew these faces; they were our neighbors or we saw them in town or at church. But when they moved it was slow and deliberate, as though the room were filled with water as clear as Boston crystal, each movement almost stilled, as though all the work it took to move in the thick, slow air was as regular as our normal movements but tonight were so slow we had time to think everything through, see ourselves as in a dream, and time stretched and allowed too much to happen.

A distinct voice in my head announced that this was a dream as there was no sense to this.

Oliver, I said. It came out on its own and sounded more than I'd wanted. What are you doing, I said.

I stood, about to take a first step.

Old Brown brought up his sabre, its point aimed at me, dancing.

You stop right there, he said. His eyes cut to his youngest son, then back.

Papa moved forward but the man I had no name for quickly brought up his rifle and laid it across Papa's chest, barring him. Papa looked down at the blue-steel barrel and then at the man holding the rifle.

Is this how you were reared, Mr. Brown, frightening women and children in the middle of the night. Like hooligans. You shame yourself.

You will not harm the women, he said. It was an announcement.

Brown met Papa's eyes, clashing fierce looks.

Not less they puts themselves into its middle, Brown said. This is about fixing some men's ideas owning other men. We have reached the point where there is no room for that way of thinking. That way of thinking is dead.

His words hung out there like a sign you couldn't avoid. In that room there were crowded almost a dozen grown people and we each followed the echo of Brown's words deep into our minds, figuring out his meaning.

Oliver, you cannot do this, I said. This is not who you are.

Old Brown kept his sword pointed at me, but his eyes, ricocheted from me to Oliver and back.

Oliver looked at me, his eyes at first dull, turned in, but then softening in degrees, and for a heartbeat I saw his impossible burden, and then the window into him closed and he lowered his eyes.

You believe you can hide from yourself, I asked. You think if you look away you aren't here, your daddy isn't here, Simon isn't here, I'm not here? This is a sad bunch that breaks into our home and stands in judgment. Have you told your daddy what you are to me and Simon? Does he know your true heart?

Oliver met my eyes and his lips formed a word but Old Brown then glared at him and it was as good as a slap, that boy dropped his eyes, his shoulders lowered, his whole body seemed to sink, like God had hammered him partway into the ground.

That is enough, said Old Brown, and he stepped forward and used the tip of his sword to sit me back down. I dropped my eyes to my feet, unable to understand, wondering if I had gone mad, wishing with all my heart I was dreaming or crows could fly indoors or we could return to Tennessee.

He is a Brown and this is God's work, that is what he does, God's work, he said. God owns his heart, not some slavers devils from Tennessee.

The air had gone out of us, a force bigger than us had stormed in and we were just things caught up in the spinning air.

The boys and Papa allowed themselves to be lead outside. I raised my head and Simon met my eyes as he neared the doorway, his eyes sad and confused and scared.

Mama remained seated, frozen, her eyes too wide, until we heard the clatter of boots leave the porch, and then she rose, as fast as a startled animal, and headed toward the door. I was right behind her.

Papa and the boys were pushed down the slope that led to the creek, away from the light that spilled out the front door. I could hear Simon saying, Oliver, what is this? Why you doing this? And the Brown boy saying, shut up, you got nothing we want to hear, and Simon saying back, but we are, are friends, we—

—He said shut up, Old Brown said. You'd best do it.

Their receding dark gray shapes joined the greater dark night and it was only their voices I heard and those too faded, seemed to be swallowed up by the night that pressed in around us.

I rushed back inside and grabbed one of the rifles and started to run by Mama toward where our men had been taken. Mama's hand snagged my arm and stopped me, spinning me around like a toy.

No, Sarah, we must stay and protect Jonah, that is our first duty, she said. I looked at her hand gripping my arm, at the rifle dangling from my other arm like a stick for poking at snakes, at the dark that wanted to suck me into its needs. The air drained out of me and I felt used up. I let the rifle drop to the dirt and Mama held me.

Mama and I stood just off the porch and held each other and we strained to see into the black but it did no good, the little moon sliver was a mere decoration hanging in the sky and gave no light worth speaking of.

Then grunts and thuds and parts of words and then something that sounded like a melon halved and then a cry like I never heard, like I never want to hear again, and then more of that awful noise, a noise I knew with the kind of certainty I refused to acknowledge and then silence and then the silence shattered by a gunshot that made Mama and me jump, the big noise echoing down the creek and up the ravines and over the prairie, and we both collapsed into each other on the ground at the foot of the porch, covering our ears, Mama making a noise I did not know could be made and then, when that noise wore itself out and we lay there entangled in our sorrow and fear, we heard horses moving away, the thick sound of hooves and the clanging of steel against steel and then it was almost quiet, the only thing I heard a roaring that at first I believed was a storm coming at us but then I recognized it as the sound of my own heart.

We did not want to go down that slope but of course after the silence grew swollen enough we could not ignore it we gathered ourselves, gave each other strength, set a lamp and descended the slope to near the creek where Papa and William and Drury and Simon were, sprawled in ways no one would willingly arrange himself, limbs angled like a twister been through, glistening dark red blood everywhere, their wounds deep and vicious and unforgiving.

There was nothing to do, they were gone to us, dead.

For as long as I would live I would end the memory of that night with the flashing red glint of light I seen in my head, the downward swing of Old Brown's sabre.

We learned after their visitation on us they went to the Wilkinson place and called out old Wilkinson and hacked him to death in front of his wife. Then they went on to James Harris's place up near Dutch Henry's and roused him and his wife and some guests. Mrs. Harris thought they were Missourians there to help them rid the area of free-staters and she started to make breakfast for the Browns, who after some confusion, announced their true intention. They then took one man out and cut him up until he died.

1960

John David

I t seemed like walking out of an afternoon movie and the sunlight knocking you off your feet, the way I came out of my dizziness watching Woody flail at his car. I scrambled to my feet and ran to the car, pulling off my jacket, and then both of us beat at the flames, which seemed to recede and surge but then we pounded it and pounded it and then the flames seemed sucked back into someplace, were gone, just like that, though plenty of thick black smoke continued to coil around under the open hood.

We stared at it for a moment and then as though cued, we each turned and leaned back against the front fenders and raised our eyes to the night's sky, as many stars as you'd ever see. I didn't want to stop looking.

I felt the car shift, heard Woody crunching on the gravel shoulder, then he said, watch yourself, and I levered away from the fender just as he crashed down the hood, sounded like a cherry bomb. His eyes were locked on something, inside the car or inside him, sliding over everything, not noticing any of it, his eyes just along for the ride as his body took command. He yanked open the driver's door and slid behind the wheel. He still hadn't looked at me. I felt like I was spying on him, I seemed so far away.

Then he surprised me, turned his head and met my stare.

You coming or you just gonna stand there and catch a ride with whoever comes along?

His voice was flat but hard as a diamond.

You think it's okay, I said. What about Dorthea, we can't leave her here.

He didn't say anything right away but his face took on his voice's stoniness.

We are gonna drive this son of a bitch home and we are gonna do it right now. I have had my fill of this night and I am taking us home. This car will get us there. I don't care if we turn into a ball of flame. I don't give a shit about the nigger. She can walk. Get in.

I put my hand on the handle but then turned and looked in the direction I'd last seen Dorthea when she'd crawled off. Nothing.

What if she's hurt, Woody? We can't leave her.

Maybe you have that problem but I do not. Now, get in or put yourself down for a midnight hike. You ain't more than fifteen miles from town.

I called out her name, heard it fade into the dark, called again, listened with all my might, and heard nothing that wasn't a regular night sound.

Well, hot damn, looky here, he said, his mouth stretching into a knife blade smile.

I looked where Woody was looking and saw Dorthea, just at the edge of our lights, walking away from us unsteadily along the shoulder, her dress unrecognizable from before, only her dark skin told me it was her.

I opened the door and sat shotgun. Woody looked at the hood while he turned the key, the motor catching right away, idle sounded rough but I reckon the carb was having some trouble breathing proper, smoke and all.

He put the car into gear and fed some gas, the rear wheels spitting some gravel as we pulled back onto the blacktop. The motor still sounded uncertain and the air was foul, oily, but nothing coming out of the vents like before.

It's that nigger's fault, Woody said. His eyes were focused on the roadway, his hands tight at two and ten on the wheel.

Woody—

—I don't wanna hear it, John David. You are only a nose behind that nigger in the blame department. We had a perfectly good plan for the night, go up and see some naked women and then go back home, simplest thing in the world, guys we know been doing it for years. Hell, my daddy and your daddy probably done it too.

I couldn't make that picture come together, but then I didn't much want to.

But, no, it couldn't be that easy for us, no, we got to ask some nigger girl to have some drinks with us and before long we've dumped our plan and are in my car headed home except we got the nigger girl with us, playing nigger music on my radio, and filling us up with nigger stories.

We were accelerating slowly, Woody not pushing it. His eyes never wavered from the road and the cones of light and Dorthea growing larger.

I think I know the solution to how I feel, said Woody. He glanced my way. Hold on tight, buddy, things are about to get bumpy.

He made a noise that I knew he'd call a laugh but no one who heard it would agree.

Woody, what are you doing, I said, noting the edge in my own voice. My stomach dropped away as we surged forward and Woody leaned forward, his chin almost resting on the steering wheel, his lips pulled back over his teeth, his eyes glistening in the light off the instruments.

Woody, I yelled.

When Woody swerved the big Buick onto the shoulder, the tires threw gravel under the car, made a racket. Dorthea's head came around and her eyes widened just as her mouth widened, and her arms came up and she stumbled backward, her arms waving, her hands opening and shutting like she was grabbing air and surprised it wouldn't hold her up.

1856

The days after were a collection of dull-colored pictures. We shuffled around, not knowing what to do. Our hearts were torn out and it seemed impossible we would ever not feel the immeasurable loss, ever not see in our dreams the unbearable things we saw as regular as sunsets.

A few kind people stopped by, brought us pies and food in baskets. They sat with us and no one would say anything for minutes and minutes, just sat there with their hands gathered in their laps, Mama dabbing at her eye or the visitor doing the same, then some one would finally say some words they'd probably heard at someone else's house, sitting around saying nothing, the kind you might normally hear at church, and then it would get quiet again and then they'd leave and we'd sit and stare at each other and wonder inside if we'd be able to continue. It seemed like a real enough question.

My insides felt ripped up and knotted up at once.

I was lost. I could not face seeing Oliver Brown again. There was nothing he could say, no possible combination of sounds that could ever make the right word to make sense of him or set things right.

I have stared at every star in the universe, night after night, asked the questions every widow asked, and quite a few more that seemed special to my situation, when your love kills your family and one of them was your love too.

I willed myself to disown myself. My insides had betrayed everything about me of any worth. I had found it possible to love a man who would later help murder my Papa and William and Drury and Simon. I knew it was something that happened after, I knew all day that fact, how could I be blamed for what someone done after, but all night a different voice reigned in my head and it tortured me with the things I should have known or paid heed to, if I was so smart.

And then things got truly knotted up.

Mama took notice after the third day I got sick. The first day took me by surprise, waking up, doing my chores, right after breakfast suddenly my insides roiling around, a bubble rushing up from deep inside. I dropped what I was doing and ran outside, made it almost to the nearest field before it erupted out of me, then me bent over, retching, holding my stomach and then wiping my mouth with my sleeve. I walked away a few feet and sat down, my back against a tree stump, and gathered my wits, wiped away sweat that was on my brow, and waited to feel better.

I had a notion but I refused to give it words.

Mama asked if I was all right and I told her I was, I'd just eaten something that didn't set with me. She said that happens and offered me a smile and we soon forgot about it.

The next morning it happened again but I wasn't caught off-guard and I slipped out a little ahead of my full sickness, walked away from the house and out of sight down by some box elders.

Mama gave me a look when I came back but she didn't say nothing and I didn't either but when she passed by me I heard her sniff and I knew she could smell it and that I hadn't fooled her a bit.

The third day, as careful as I was, when I came back inside, she took my arm and pulled me back out and walked me off from the house like we were gonna inspect the garden.

You want to tell me what's going on, she said.

I started to say that nothing was going on, I just wasn't feeling good, but her eyes bore into me and scratched around inside my head, peeked into every place that could be peeked into and I knew she knew and that my lying to her would do no good. But I still wasn't ready to admit I knew anything about anything.

I been sick, I said.

I can see that, she said. That ain't what I'm asking you about.

I wanted to look off at the hills and the woods and the rising sun and then say something smart or say something that circled what instead had to be said but much to my surprise I burst into tears and collapsed at her feet. I was as astonished by myself as if I'd suddenly grown extra legs and a mane and become a horse.

At first she let me lie there like a puddle and cry, my whole self shaking as though a thunderstorm was tearing me apart, but then she came down and joined me and held me and patted my shoulders and rubbed my back and cooed like a mourning dove into my hair.

Some secrets are too big to let out and too big to keep inside and there I was, the weight of my family's shame and the dark confused thrill of my love made whole, this baby inside the secret itself.

At first I barely nodded my head when Mama asked me questions. No one wanted to put it into words, she no doubt thinking that if I didn't say anything perhaps she was imagining things; me, if she didn't say anything perhaps there was nothing to see, nothing to notice, to know about, to make real with its names.

That nonsense wore off as I grew and settled into my term and we worked out our new lives. We refused to leave or give up or even lose our crop and we worked every day that summer from when the sun first lighted the sky to when we could not longer see our work and we got through.

Later I told myself I'd fallen from grace. Just as I once lay awake staring into the thick dark over my bed struggling against my feelings, I now embraced the world in a new way.

Later still, I'd look back and on those days when the pain of loss overwhelmed me I'd lay the whole history at the foot of my reading the New Testament and only understanding the chapters about love.

I had sought love, wanted love, wanted to repay the world with love. I accepted my blessings and desired to erase my debt.

I stopped noticing the crows, turning my back to them when I heard them cawing in the maples and cottonwoods, spun away if

I caught one taking wing off to the side, ignored their chatter, and told myself it was nonsense, the result of some girl's fever, some silly conceit I had due to having nothing better to do than to make tall tales of my life.

Why not fly?

The danger isn't falling to earth; the danger is seeing too much.

People figured it out all on their own, or put together versions that served well enough, added it up and totaled an answer they were convinced was right. Gifts showed on our porch and no one ever left a note. Clothes for a boy child, corn bread or small cakes, a baby blanket, the fabric pieces vaguely familiar, like we'd seen them on some folks in town on Saturdays past, a baby rattle made from a tiny gourd.

Mama and me thought it came from some Brown or another. Maybe even Oliver, though he knew better than to show at our door. There are simply some angers that prayer falls short of soothing, some pains only worsened by time, not healed.

I reeled from my black anger, my fevered desire to take Papa's rifle and march over to the Brown place and make that boy look into that barrel until enough light filled his eyes to show him what was coming. And then I'd pull the trigger and watch his head fly apart like a thousand startled cardinals.

I awoke ashamed for the thoughts I allowed to creep into my head in the middle of the night when I'd wake up and look at the stars and imagine joining them, when I tried to remember what I'd heard about some herbs, when I wondered how far away could I get. When I plotted murder, of one kind or another.

Then one day I just woke up determined, no other word for it, and when Mama was out, at the well or tending to the livestock, I pulled the chest of drawers away from the back wall and got Papa's knife and carved what I wanted into the back. I'd know it was there and that was enough. I had to get it out of me and this seemed like the only way I could talk about it, scratching my heart's words into that wood.

Our brother was gone but here in this wood he would be joined with me.

It could not be talked about, there just weren't no words possible for what I'd done, for what had happened, but even for that it was bursting from me like a dandelion exploding its seeds into the summer wind. I knew what people would think, what they'd believe they knew if I said nothing, if I kept it locked inside, and even though I knew that was wrong—wrong in fact and wrong of me to permit it to be known as fact—when sat down next to the other thing it seemed like something I could live with and pass along as fact, no matter what tongues would wag at every opportunity.

There was hardly a thought since that did not include or lead to Simon's name in my head. What I told myself was that he lived on through me, that we'd been combined.

I never saw the Brown boy unless we saw each other across a street in town and then we'd each look away. We'd become opposites as black and white, and I know I had nothing to say to him or rather I had too much and I knew that once I started I'd still be pouring it out of me on my deathbed so I said nothing and thought nothing and after a while I saw nothing, he ceased to be in my mind, he no longer walked my dreams or argued with me or showed me his smiles. No, it was never to be again, that's what I told myself every night just before I counted the stars.

1955

The roof of the Forty-seven Olds coupe was cool against my back as I lay there, my arms spread out like counterweights, my legs slightly spread as though I was tacked up there, a child butterfly beneath the countless numbers of winking stars scattered across the deep black cloth of July's summer sky. The air was still hot and damp the way Kansas summer night air can be, the kind of night where you lie atop your sheets and if your skin touches other skin it sticks with the perspiration caught between them like a poor man's glue.

I was out on top of the car parked along the curb in front of our house because the steel was cool and I didn't want to lie in the yard and then have to deal with the tiny red chiggers that seemed to live in our lawn as numerous as the blades of grass.

Hardly any air moved that night but I didn't care. I was locked onto some star or some group of stars, my ignorance of the constellations, of the stars as separate from planets, was as complete as my ignorance of what made the air hot or what made the summer nights almost impossible to sleep through without awakening sweaty and feverish.

God was up there, I just knew it, and if I stared long enough, if I focused on the right stars, I'd see some sign of the route to where he lived. Or maybe I'd only catch a UFO skittering across the sky. Or maybe just a falling star sliding in its fast arc across one corner before it flared into nothingness.

I took to looking for falling stars, of which there were plenty, and UFOs, of which there seemed to be none, a fact that frustrated me as much as my inability to float upward into the night. Each falling star began at the edges of my vision, as though it was a rule that none could begin its flight in full sight, and the sudden movement of bright light raised in me the false hope that this dancing light would be the coming of something strange and frightful, though it never was anything more than a streak of light cut across the white-dotted sky, and then, maybe, an unexpected flare as the meteor burnt out in the lower atmosphere.

On other evenings, I'd join some kids on the lawn where we watched the night sky for flying saucers. Farmers and truck drivers and even sheriffs' deputies said they'd seen things that shouldn't be there, lights that grew to the size of space ships.

But no one seemed to believe them, or at least my folks didn't, their comments at the dinner table after they'd each read the afternoon paper ranged from mild amusement to outright scorn that people could be so easily confused by what had to be such simple occurrences as weather balloons or swamp gas or lights oddly reflected into the sky. They thought that people who saw such things were crazed or drunk or some kind of simpleton; or maybe it was just that if you saw something that was out of the ordinary, the smart thing to do was to keep your mouth shut about it since nothing in their experience or knowledge permitted visitations from other planets.

The truth was, what I really wanted was to have the same visitation that came upon John Brown. I wanted my blood to boil as his did. I wanted courage.

There was a long list of things I needed courage for, but I knew the first thing I needed to do was to talk to Sharon Marie. I had to tell her what I was pretty sure she already knew, that I was too frightened by my feelings and that I wished I was a better person but I wasn't and that's what I'll tell her first thing next time I see her. And then I hoped she'd talk me out of it.

When school started I went looking for her but she wasn't in our class and no one had seen her.

I asked Jamie if he'd seen Sharon Marie and he gave me a look, his head shaking back and forth just the tiniest bit.

She gone, he said. Her family moved to Kansas City, looking for work.

Gone, I said. Even I could hear my voice make a sound somewhere between a question and a cry.

I did not see her again, my words to her lost in my head where they haunted me like angry birds.

1859

The Brown boy got himself killed at Harpers Ferry. What family he still had in the territory didn't ever say anything to me about it one way or the other.

His death only confused matters in my heart, some of it a kind of celebration though I knew that thinking came from parts buried deep in places where no light would ever reach; some of me mourned the passing of a love though that word was never allowed to settled down next to that boy's name ever again; and some of me wrestled with the argument that it did not matter, that it was a stranger who'd got himself killed back east and it had nothing to do with my life.

About a month or so after word reached Kansas that Brown and his followers had attacked Harpers Ferry, I received a letter, handed to me when I visited town for a sack of flour. The old man who ran the store thrust it toward my face, his expression as sour as a green persimmon, Here, he said, his voice a dulled saw blade.

I looked at him and at the letter he dangled in my face. I matched his eyes with my own brand of sour and snatched the letter like a housefly caught midair. I pivoted and marched out, the letter held tightly at my side, my eyes focused on a kind of nothingness that seemed to recede as my feet took me back to my wagon.

I tucked it inside my dress and did not look at it until I was home and even then I did not open it and read it until I'd gone around back of the outbuilding and sat in its shade, the day's heat an arm's length away.

I read it and then I read it again and then I made myself read it a third time. He knew he'd owned me with his words before and now he wanted his words to erase his actions as though it was as simple as dragging a cloth across a blackboard, soaking up chalked words like spilled goat milk, nothing left but a crusty dampness to hint at what the world had witnessed.

As words go, he did not know enough to make them do his bidding; he certainly did not know enough about me to expect I'd carry some of his words' burden, that I'd see his letter as a hand reaching back to me, asking for my own to help him live with what he done to me and mine.

I wasn't having it, not that day and not any of those that followed. I was done with things that could be so easily twisted into knots by sounds arranged like jewels to bedazzle the brain. From this point all else is banned from my life if I cannot touch it or taste it or feel its silent embrace. Words do not count for more than the simplest of things; they are ill-equipped to support the weight of what hides in our hearts.

I lived my life and I endured looks that said whatever my mind at the time believed they said, looks that cut away when I stared back, daring the person to voice what their eyes said. No one had the courage to say what was in their eyes, but it was as plain to me as if they'd painted signs and worn them around their necks, like those drawn pictures you'd see in the magazines and broadsheets, their words spelled out inside bubbles.

Truth was, opinions of my conduct were as common as grasshoppers in August, and they were of two camps, none of them generous or forgiving. I was the Brown boy's whore or worse.

Women detoured when they saw me in town, my baby in my arms or later tagging along at my skirt. He was a lonely boy, later taunted by the other children, whose parents stubbornly refused to let them play with my boy. He grew up with his uncle Jonah and me and with what we built.

It weren't never his fault. He knew the air became thin around townsfolk, but he said nothing, asked nothing, and seemed to grow into the silence carved out by the others. It suited him enough to take each day separate from the others, yesterday's talk lost in night's passage. In that way he was unlike his namesakes, two boys whose heads were filled with notions, their souls tangled up with the world's troubles. But then even though my little Simon Oliver didn't ever know his daddies he had me to point him in the right direction.

1960

Dorthea

I knew I was dead. It was the most certain thing I'd ever felt. I heard that big car and I wheeled around and it was like a house of light falling on me. There was nothing to do but pay attention to what it would be like.

And then in a blink the wall of light jerked left and flashed by me, inches away, my eyes seeing them two white boys, all their hands on the steering wheel, their mouths open and them looking at each other with terrible things in their eyes, and then it was by me and there was an explosion of noises as the car smashed nose first into the ditch, and dirt and water and junk filled the air, and then the car quivered to a stop and white smoke boiled up from underneath. It had happened so fast it seemed the car had passed right through me, that I was already a ghost.

I don't know how long I stood in that spot. I remember looking at my hands and feet and thinking, you're still here, girl.

Soon I thought to look at the wrecked car, saw right off the one driving was halfway out the windshield. The part stretched out over the hood looked like someone had dipped him in red paint.

I stumbled around the back of the car, saw the other door was hanging open and the other boy, John David, was outside, spread there like a doll thrown out the window of another car. He made a noise.

I scrambled down the ditch, crawled over to him and rolled him over, out of the muddy water. His face was black with mud and that smoke, his eyes pale and wide. I didn't see no blood except some dribbled down his chin, but he didn't look right.

He said some things, but I couldn't hear at first, a roar like a twister inside my head, and blood bubbled out with each word. I bent my ear to his lips.

He raised his hand and touched my face and said some girl's name like asking me a question and then shut his eyes.

GRATITUDES & ACKNOWLEDGEMENTS

Much praise and thank-yous to: Charlotte Gusay, my longtime friend and agent; she has always been there and worked her heart out; Jane Levine, simply the best editor and copyeditor and partner; all the other editors/writers who believed in my work and troubled to publish it or support it (James Vowell, Steve Erickson, Lou Mathews, David A. Schabes); David Rhoades, my high school English teacher who put me on the trail of cool writing; Pete Genovese, my old pal and hero; my other hero, Dan Raphael, the best underknown poet in America; Leonard Durso, Jim Powell, and Gordon Anderson, founders of Intellectuals & Liars, the best literary bookstore Los Angeles ever lost; and Philip F. O'Connor, who saw what I didn't.